The Land of

Immortalis

Chapter 1

Cap runs as fast as he can through the trees. The fire rages behind him, nipping at his heels. He stops to breathe, and looks back. The trees flame up with each passing moment. His feet ache, his lungs hurt, and his energy is about spent. He must go on though. A bullet flies by, followed by the report of a gun. It is a large warning that it is time for him to go, quickly. He takes off running. The flames are closing in, as well as his enemy. He searches through the trees, looking for any way out.

Off to the right, he sees a clearing. Through the heat waves there is a snow capped mountain in the distance. He begins to sprint towards it, and then stops suddenly. Something doesn't feel right about it. He hears another gun shot, and bolts forward into the waves. He trips and rolls down a steep hill. Landing he looks back. There is no fire, no trees. There is only a cave on top of a hill.

The ground moves underneath him. He watches as the boulders above the cave fall and seals off his escape route. Exhausted, he falls to his knees. He closes his eyes, and tries to think back to what got him here. But he's too tired, and he now has to find shelter, water, and food. He spots a cluster of trees in the distance, and starts walking towards them. As he sets his pace, he looks back. "How did this happen to me?" he wonders out loud.

Cap walks on. He knows he needs shelter and water. The grove of trees ahead of him looked like the perfect place. They looked like they were far away, but they are getting closer with each step. The snowcapped mountains far to the east are his guides to make sure he walks a straight path.

He looks up at the sun. From its location he guesses it is almost noon. He walks on, hopeful, yet worried. He is in a land he didn't know, around terrain that was completely unfamiliar. He thought back, he had no idea what had happened, but he was alive, and for that he could thank God.

Arriving at the grove, he sees that it is actually two separate groves. They're separated by a small creek running in between them. He smiles at his good fortune. Here there is shelter, water, and a good possibility of food. Right now, he couldn't be happier.

He kneels down by the clear cool creek and drinks greedily. He never imagined he was this thirsty. Standing up he looks at his reflection in the water. His sandy brown hair is soaked with sweat. His face is covered with black streaks of smoke and stubble, and his lean muscular figure shows signs of fatigue. He sits down and looks around. He needs rest, and a shelter to rest under.

He looks to his right, and notices a log that has fallen in the not too distant past, still covered with green leaves. Noticing the potential for shelter, he then sets out to find his next need, food. Cap walks around the grove looking for some sort of way to get food. Near the edge of the creek, close to the end of the grove, he finds a raspberry bush. Taking off his shirt, he fills it up with as many berries as he can pick. Going back to his log, he sits and gorges his meal. Finishing he washes himself and his shirt in the creek. He then swiftly starts breaking branches and places them over the hanging limbs of the log. He steps back and looks at his work. It's only a make shift lean-to, but it's going to be home for at least one night. He crawls in, and sweeps out all the leaves and pine needles from the ground. Exhausted, he lies down, and quickly falls asleep…

***

His eyes fly open. It is very dark outside. There is no light within the shelter. Through the branches, he can see that someone is moving around the area. He suddenly realizes that help may just walk on by. He sits up to call out, but is suddenly pushed back down, a hand placed over his mouth.

"Settle down son," an older man's voice whispers, "You don't want to let your presence be known right now."

Extremely confused and curious, questions pile upon themselves as he lays still, the man's hand still over his mouth. It felt as if time stood still as they waited for who was ever outside to leave. Then, out of the black night, a screech that that is almost deafening, and what sounds like a stampede that seems to be running.

The old man lifted his hand and spoke, just stay here, and be quiet. I'll go check it out."

He crawls out without a sound. Cap just looks out the branches at his new companion. He can only see the man's figure, but that is enough. He could tell he wore a cowboy hat. He stood straight, at what looks like six feet tall. The man looks at everything very meticulously. He's studying everything that seems to be invisible to Cap. Cap studied the man, trying to learn as much as he could about him. The man disappears into the darkness. Extremely curious, Cap hesitantly steps into the open night air.

The man reappears with wood in his arms. "It's goin' to be daylight soon," the man says to him, "Sit down, and I'll light a fire and make some coffee."

Cap sat on a stump and watched the man build a fire. He begins by striking flint with steel, and blowing on the tinder, lights a small fire. The flame takes, and the man adds larger sticks to it. Cap just looks on in wonder.

"It won't be big, but it'll be enough for coffee," the man says.

"Thank you, sir," Cap tells him. With the fire lighting up the night, he can now get a good look at the man. He looked to be in his early fifties, with gray hair, and some gray showing in the man's beard.

"Don't mention it. I don't know how you got here, but you

shouldn't bed down out here at night. There are creatures out in that night that would consider you a snack. Just a friendly warning. My name's Logan. If you want, you can stick around with me for a while." the man tells him.

"I would appreciate that a lot," Cap answers, "My name is Casey, but everyone calls me Cap. I'm not sure if I can repay you for all of this."

"I didn't ask you to," Logan tells him, "but trust me. From what I've seen around this place, the company would be good."

"And what is this place," Cap asks him.

"The locals have a fitting name for it. I just call it black magic. There's things here that can't be explained." He hands Cap a tin cup, and pours him some coffee, then turns around away from the fire. Cap taking this as a sign that he was done talking, quietly sips his coffee and stares at the fire.

They sit silent. As the first rays of light pierce the night sky, Logan turns around and kicks out the fire. He then douses it with the rest of the coffee. He takes Cap's cup, then puts the pot and cups in a small leather pack.

Placing it on his back, he turns to Cap and says, "Well, Cap. If we leave now, we can make it to the road in a couple of hours. Hopefully, we can get to Avalon before nightfall."

Cap gets an amused look on his face, "They have a town named Avalon? I can't wait to see this."

Logan just turns and walks to the north, with Cap following slightly to his right. Logan seems to be following an invisible trail. Cap just follows along quietly, just enjoying the cool morning breeze. He looks off to the east as the sun rises, bathing the land in a majestic blanket of red. The clouds above grabbed the sunlight and blended the colors into beautiful shades of white, gray, red, and green. To the west, he could see the dark purple of night retreat from its brighter brother.

As the light allows more and more visibility, Cap begins to notice a few things. The grass was softer and greener than he has ever seen before. What surprises him more is that he cannot see a single weed in sight. The trees seem to grow straight towards the sky, without any flaws. He is now more confused than ever. How could such a place exist? Better yet, how is it that he got here? Running from his enemy and the heat from a forest fire in the mountains to here? It doesn't make any sense!

Cap searched his brain, looking for any explanation while Logan walks on silently. Something about this place bothers him. He doesn't know what or how, just that it does. He just can't seem to put his finger on it. He could feel the mystery, but also a sense of fear all around him.

Logan suddenly stops, and motions for Cap to get down on the ground. Logan gets down as well, and then begins to high crawl to the top of a small hill. He pokes his head over, then motions for Cap to join him. Cap copies Logan's high crawl to the top of the hill. When he looks over the top below, he gasps in surprise.

What he sees is nothing more than unexplainable! Right at the bottom of the hill stands a pure white winged horse. "My God," Cap whispers, "It's a pterippus!"

Logan chuckles a bit and whispers, "I said this place was full of black magic. But there is some good magic here too."

"This can't be real!" Cap exclaims, "The pterippus is a mythical creature. It's not supposed to even exist!"

"Yeah, that may be," Logan says, "But right there it is. Plain as day. This place doesn't seem to believe in the impossible. You and I see a winged horse, a pterippus you called it, that's not supposed to be alive. But 'round here, this is an everyday occurrence."

Cap stands up in disbelief. The pterippus looks up, opens its wings and flies off to the North, the sun glinting off of its brilliant white coat. Cap just stands and stares as it flies away. He is nothing short of mesmerized by what he has just seen. Logan stands up, and places his hand on Cap's shoulder, bringing him out of his trance. Cap looks at Logan, eyes wide, mouth dropped open.

"Relax," Logan tells him, "I'll try to explain as best as I can as soon as we get to the road. If that doesn't help you out any, you will have to wait till we get to Avalon."

Cap just looks at him stupefied. Logan laughs then motions for him to follow along. Cap follows Logan obediently as he begins to walk to the North again. Cap's eyes are wide open, alert for any movement. His senses are tuned to the slightest, well, anything. He searches for anything that might seem out of place. But here that could be anything. This place just isn't normal at all. Once again the question enters his mind. What is this place?

Cap and Logan top a hill, and below them is a road paved in gold. In between them and the road is a herd of deer. Logan mouths 'Stay here' to Cap. They kneel down, and Logan pulls off his pack. He pulls out a pistol. What looks like a Colt .45 to Cap. Logan then begins to crawl slowly down the hill.

Logan moves down the hill silently. He disappears into the tall grass. Cap tries to follow the movements of the grass with his eyes, but is looking at nothing but grass and deer. Cap can't do anything but watch and wait. Just when he begins to doze off, he hears a gun shot, and then sees one deer fall to the ground as the others run off.

Logan stands up from out of nowhere. He waves for Cap to join him. Cap stands up and walks down the hill. Logan has the deer skinned by the time he gets to him. Logan had the skin laid out and was placing cuts of meat onto it. Cap noticed that he was only taking the best cuts.

Confused, he opens his mouth to ask, but changes his mind.

"It's for a family in Avalon," Logan says suddenly, "they need some help, and this will help feed them for a couple days."

Cap doesn't say a word. Just helps wrap the meat in the hide. He then picks up the bundle, his own little way of helping out, and walks to the road. They get to the road, and stop. Logan points east.

"This way to Avalon. If we keep a steady pace, we should get there before nightfall." Logan tells him.

"And what town is west of here?" Cap asks.

"No one goes west of here," Logan explains, "The only thing that's west of here is death. Trust me when I say you don't want to go that way. There are many creatures that way that only want blood. Death would not be painless, and it would not be quick."

Cap's face shows fear, "Alright then. East good, west bad. Got it."

"Don't take it lightly," Logan states, "I'm not joking when I say that way lies death. Many good men have ventured off that way, and very few have returned."

Cap just stood there silent. It's hard for him to believe, but as of right now, he doesn't know what to believe. He is starting to believe that everything he knows and everything he's been taught can be thrown out the window. But what does he believe? If nothing he knows exists, that makes him a new born child in this place. Something, anything, must be the same though. He searches his mind for just one thing he can hold on to.

Logan watches his confusion. "Relax kid. I felt the same way when I first got here. The locals call this place Immortalis. And I can tell you, it fits its name well. Everything is clean. There are no sicknesses; men don't seem to die from natural causes. Of course, there's more than plenty of unnatural causes that don't give nature a chance. That's about all I can tell you for now. I'll try to get some more information for you when we get to town."

Cap's mind races with questions. He's not quite sure if he's ready to ask them of Logan, nor is he ready for the answers. The old man seems to only speak and explain what he wants when he wants. It's something Cap can understand. It's something he's not willing to push.

They walk on in silence, for what felt like hours to Cap. He couldn't help but feel amazed at the road he is walking on. When he saw it for the first time, he only thought that it looked like gold. Now, he realizes with surprise, that it is gold. Amazed, yet confused, he couldn't help but wonder what kind of civilization would waste a major part of their economy on such a simple road. It is just one more thing that gives him uneasiness about this area, this place, this land of wonder, dread, and impossibilities.

This thought brought him to another. How could a place like this exist? The impossible is the norm here, but that doesn't mean that all the impossible should occur. Yet, with all the impossibilities, the normal possibilities in life are still here. For all that, there has to be something that evens it all out. Everything is based off of balance. So, the big question is where is the balance? In a world where there are no limits on impossibilities, there must be something that balances the normal from the abnormal. What that could be, he doubts he can figure it out right now.

He looks at both sides of the road. He sees nothing but green grass and rolling hills. Up ahead, in the distance, he can see a curve in the road. Bushes line both sides of it. He can see flowers of many colors blooming throughout the curve. As they near it, a flock of birds flies into the air, and leaves the area swiftly. Cap suddenly gets an uneasy feeling. Something doesn't feel right, and his pace slows because of it. He looks at Logan, but Logan doesn't seem fazed.

Logan notices Cap slowing down. "There are sentries posted at this curve. That's probably why the birds flew off quickly. There isn't anything to worry about," Logan assures him.

As they approach the bend, Cap begins to tense up. Logan notices, but says nothing. Nonchalantly, Logan pulls his pistol out without Cap noticing. They enter the curve, and Cap's senses seem to triple in sensitivity. He can hear the breeze through the leaves. He feels like he can see every detail of the road, every leaf, and every petal. He can smell every flower, and something bitter, almost copper that he can't place. He searches for anything that could be wrong. There seems to be nothing, but the uneasiness doesn't go away. They get through without incident. Cap looks back, that's when he sees it. A pool of blood and an arm sticking out of the bushes!

"Get down!" Logan yells at him.

Cap turns around to see Logan pointing his pistol. Cap falls to the ground as the first shot is fired. He rolls over and notices that behind him is six disfigured beings running towards them, one now lying dead on the ground. Logan fires again and one more falls down. He throws a knife to Cap, "Go for the head!" he yells.

With that, the things were upon them. The four rush towards Cap. The first one reaches for him, and he slices the hand off instinctively. The being screams a high pitch shrill in pain. The sound stuns Cap as the other three get a hold of him. He comes to his senses as each one grabs a different extremity. Both legs and his left arm are now held. Panicking, he starts punching the one holding his arm with the hilt of his knife. He hit's the thing harder and harder, but the creature doesn't seem fazed. He turns the knife around and stabs the thing in the eye. The creature shrieks as Cap pulls out the knife, and then falls dead to the ground. He turns his attention to the two at his feet. Logan runs in and kicks one off of him

The thing rose like a cat, and Logan engages it in battle

immediately. Cap doesn't have time to watch. He begins to kick the creature off of his leg, and then tries to stab it in the head. His blade found dirt as the creature rolls over. It gets up and begins to circle Cap cautiously.

Cap studies the creature, looking for the perfect opportunity. It has pale green skin around what seems like a human body, but there wasn't much human about it. Its clothes were tattered and torn. Its hands and feet look like it has claws. The creature runs at Cap all of a sudden, shrieking as it ran. Cap just stands still, and then with a fast thrust, shoves the blade of his knife into the creature's mouth, and through the back of its head. Placing his foot on the creature's chest, he pushes it off the blade, and watches it fall. Tense and ready for anything, Cap spins around, searching for what might be next.

Logan walks up to him, "Not bad for your first encounter." He slaps him on the back, and reloads his pistol.

"What the hell are those things?!" Cap half yells, half asks.

"They're zombies. They are the undead slaves of the creatures in the west," Logan answers.

"And what sadistic being would enslave the dead?"

"I don't know, and I don't want to know. Anything that has the power to raise and enslave the dead is something I don't want to meet."

Cap nods his head in agreement. He takes a look round, letting his nerves calm after the violence. A question begins to form in his head. As he ponders it, he realizes that it is something that he must ask.

"Logan, do you have any idea why they were coming after us? I mean, was it us? Or were we just in the wrong place at the wrong time?"

"I'm not sure. I've never been attacked like that before. It's different, but nothing I'm goin' to worry about. At least, not for now, anyway."

Cap stays quiet as Logan picks up the deer hide and meat. They are about to start walking when they hear a high pitched shriek from the north. On a hill they can see a line of zombies stopping at the top of it.

"I think that's our cue to go," Cap says.

"That would be a big understatement, it's time to run," Logan responds.

They watch as one zombie points at them and then shrieks loudly. All the zombies begin to run at them with amazing speed. Cap and Logan turn and run as fast as they can. Cap looks back, and notices that the zombies are closing in on them fast. Logan looks back, and then begins to run faster. There's just too many to fight, Cap thinks. He can hear the zombies shriek and stop running. Just then a gust of wind hits them from above, along with the whinny of a horse. Looking up, he sees the pterippus above them. The flying steed flies ahead, and lands in front of them.

Logan runs to it, "Get on!" he yells as he drops the meat. Logan jumps onto the animal, Cap following his lead. Cap doesn't more than sit down when the pterippus jumps into the air, the zombies shrieking in frustration at their loss.

As they fly east, Logan turns to Cap and says, "They must be after us. Alright, now I'm worried. They've never been in a group that large before. That's very odd."

Cap relaxes as he watches the zombies fade into the distance. So far, he's thanking God for his very fortunate luck. He takes a deep breath, closes his eyes, and enjoys the flight.

As the wind whips by his face, he looks down to see a surreal sight of the ground. It doesn't even look real. Everything looks small, almost toy like in appearance. If it wasn't for the feel of the wind, and the warmth of the sun on his face, he would believe that he was dreaming. Who at home would believe that he was riding a flying horse!

He soaks in the surroundings, breathing the cool air. For the first time in a long while, he's able to relax. His stomach jumps into his throat as the pterippus begins a quick descent. Pulling its wings closer to its body, the horse dives towards the ground at a remarkable speed. Fear grips Cap's heart as he sees the ground rising before him. With precision timing, the pterippus spreads its wings, almost stopping in midair. It hovers in the air for a moment, and then glides to the surface. It prances lightly as it lands.

Logan and Cap get off of the pterippus, each petting and thanking the horse in their own way. The horse shakes, and then takes off, leaving its shadow around them for a brief moment, before becoming a dot in the sky.

Logan turns to Cap, "Well, that was different."

Cap looks at Logan questioningly, "Different?"

Logan just smiles, "I've been here for a while now. I've never had one of those horses let me ride them. Let alone just let me come near them."

"Hmm, interesting," is the only thing Cap can say.

"We better get going," Logan says, "We still have a couple of miles to go, and Avalon needs to be warned about this. Zombies grouped that large can only mean something terribly bad is going on."

Cap just looks at Logan, "I'll have to take your word for it. When it comes to this place, I'm clueless."

Logan laughs out loud and waves for Cap to follow as he begins to walk. They follow the golden road to the top of a hill. What Cap sees takes the breath out of him. Ahead on the road he can see the city of Avalon. A walled city unlike anything he's ever seen before. Centered on a peninsula that extends to the middle of a large lake, the walls are raised high, and in the center a large castle. The golden road, from what he could see, went right through the city. Right up to the gate at the wall, and what seems to leave directly behind it.

"There she is, Avalon," Logan says.

Cap just stares in awe. They continued to walk the road, across the bridge and directly to the gate. Two guards dressed in medieval sentry attire stand waiting for them.

"Hello boys," Logan greets them.

They both look at Cap, but the one on the left speaks first, "Greetings, Logan," The soldier speaks in a deep Welsh accent, "Who is this with you?"

"I found this boy off the road after the quake," Logan explains.

The sentry on the right's eyes grow wide, "Is it he?"

"Now you know I don't put no stock in that," Logan answers, "But I do have urgent news to tell the knights. May we pass?"

"Yes, Yes. They will be interested in what you have to say," the one on the left says. The two sentries part to opposite sides, and allow them through.

"Logan? What were they talking about? Who is 'he'?" Cap asks. Logan just looks at Cap and smiles.

Chapter 2

Luke awakes in a cave, almost buried in dust and debris. His head hurts. He touches his forehead, and winces with pain. He looks at his fingers in the dim light, and plainly sees blood. Rage fills his stiff body. 'He did this to me,' he thinks angrily.

His thoughts race back, remembering the chase. He fired many times, but couldn't seem to hit his target. He chased his prey into the mountain forest. He had almost lost him in the forest fire. He fired his pistol at him a few more times, but couldn't seem to ever hit the moving target. It is almost like fate wouldn't allow him.

He remembered following him into what looked like a clearing. Suddenly, a flashback hits him. Memories of the earth shaking, dust flying thicker than fog, and then the falling of rocks. He shakes the thoughts out of his head, despite the throbbing. He stands and stretches, looking towards the light outside.

He yells out loud, "He did this to me! And he will pay!" Now set with his goal, but unsure of how to go through with it, he sets off to get out of the cave. He walks towards the light. Climbing over boulders, and choking on the dust filled air, he arrives to what should be the opening of the cave. Disappointed at seeing the opening blocked by a large boulder, he begins looking for a different way out. There is no other light in the cave. Sensing his death, he tries not to panic.

He frantically begins searching around again, but to no avail. Fear begins to take over his anger. Then with a burst of energy, he throws himself at the boulder. It moved! Digging his heels in, he pushes with all of his strength. It budges a small amount, and then it won't move at all. Luke pushes harder again and again, but it won't move anymore.

Panic begins to set in again. He begins punch, and even kicks the boulder. The adrenalin in his body begins to surge. Anger and frustration build up to unprecedented amounts within him. With an amazing amount of strength and power, he anchors his feet, places his back against the boulder, and shoves.

Outside the cave, clumps of dirt begin to crumble under the weight of the boulder. Smaller rocks begin to roll down the hill beneath. Luke can feel the boulder begin to move. Pulling all his energy and fury together, he pushes with more force than he believed he ever had. There's one rock holding the boulder in place. With Luke's final push, the weight of the boulder and Luke's own energy, forces the rock into the ground.

He falls backward as the boulder gives way. The boulder rolls down the hill roughly, causing the cave to shake. Rocks from the ceiling begin to fall. Luke gets up quickly and jumps out of the cave, scared that he might get trapped within the eternal tomb again. He lands hard and begins to roll down the steep hill.

He stops rolling, and just lays there. It takes him a few moments to realize that his heart is beating rapidly, and that he is gasping for air. He coughs up some phlem, spitting it out quickly. He notices that it's mostly mud that he spits. Forcing himself up, he can feel his exhaustion, and every muscle in his body is telling him to lie back down. He must begin moving though; his very survival depends on it.

Forcing himself to his feet, he stands straight up and looks around. 'Which way would Cap have gone?' he thought to himself. Looking at the sun for direction, he looks east, and sees a grove of trees in the distance. He looks west, and vaguely sees the outlines of mountains.

"Now which way?" he asks out loud, "The tree grove is closer, but Cap would know that. He must have gone west. He knows I'm following. He'll try to lose me."

Luke turns and begins walking to the west, never looking back.

Had he looked around a bit, he would have noticed Cap's tracks heading east. But with new resolve, he continues forward. Bound and determined that he won't quit till he finds the man he despises, he quickens his pace.

He looks for signs of water and food. With the mountains ahead of him, he should be able to locate a river or stream. The air around him was warm, but he could see snow a top the mountain chain through the setting sun. Stopping to rest, he takes another look around. With night coming on, he must find a place to rest. He looks all around the sky for any signs of a storm. Seeing nothing, and feeling no change in temperature in the slow breeze, he decides to take refuge under a lone tree to the south.

He quickens his walking, anxious to rest his weary muscles. The tree rises before him, and he reaches for its trunk, too tired to stand any longer. Lowering himself to the ground, he sits and catches his breath. With the last rays of light, he notices a small stream. He crawls to it and drinks deeply. Satisfied, he goes back to the tree and falls soundly asleep…

***

He awakes suddenly. The night is dark with no stars, and no moon. Just pitch black. He looks around, but darkness is all he sees. Moon light begins to show as clouds begin to part. He looks forward, and freezes in fear. In front of him he sees a tall figure, fully cloaked in a tattered robe. What really installs fear in him is that it's floating, not standing!

He rolls over quickly, and begins to run. He stops abruptly, the creature floating in front of him. He darts right, just to be stopped again. He tries to go left, but is halted in the same way. He turns around quickly, but the creature is waiting for him. He looks behind him, but sees no one or anything there.

"Wha-What do you want?" Luke manages to stammer.

The creature points a ghastly finger at him and hisses, "You."

Luke slowly walks backwards. The creature moves forward,

keeping pace with Luke. Luke's back hits the tree, and the creature bursts forward suddenly. Enveloping Luke in its cloak, it flies past the tree, and heads west to the mountains.

Chapter 3

Cap awakes on the hard floor of the tavern, with his head pounding. Logan had left him there, in the care of the barkeep when he went to speak with the knights. To Cap's surprise, everyone was cheerful, even as the rumors of Logan's news spread through the town. Many speculations flowed just as easily as the ale. It also seemed that everyone that entered the tavern last night felt obligated to buy Cap a drink. He had tried to refuse. He had none of the money they use to buy his own drinks, nor could he return any of the favors. They wouldn't listen to his protests though, insisting that he accept. Of course he didn't want to insult anyone, so he had accepted. That is where he made his mistake. The last thing he remembered was joking with a couple of the locals about "The Prophecy", and that it may have finally come to pass.

He places his hands to his forehead, trying to slow the pounding within. After lying like that for a few moments, he sits up and looks around. He can see people lying on the floor all over the place. 'God? Please forgive me for my stupidity last night!' he silently prays. Then his intelligence slowly brings the dawn of realization to him. "Oh good God! What happened?" he says out loud.

The sound of laughter brings him straight to his feet. Behind him, Logan and the barkeep are laughing, unable to hold it in. Although, Cap could see that they were trying.

"Go ahead and let it out," Cap tells them, "I'm sure I deserve it." They just look at each other, and then begin to laugh harder. Cap waits, staring at them, turning red with embarrassment.

For what seems like hours, though it's only a few minutes, they finally calm down. "Are you done?" Cap asks.

Logan answers, "We will be shortly. Just as soon as you put some clothes on."

Cap looks dumbfounded for a moment, and then looks down at himself. He sees that he is only in his boxers. "AH, SNAP!" he exclaims, then begins to search frantically for his clothes. While he is searching for his clothing, Logan and the barkeep began discussing something. Cap looks over at the two, trying to remember what happened last night. He remembers meeting the barkeep, being a little intimidated at the unusual size of the man. He was at least six feet four inches tall, maybe 250 pounds or more, and all of it muscle. As he pieces his clothing together, and gets dressed, he realizes that the man had to be that strong. All the tables and chairs were made of solid oak. He vaguely remembers admiring the craftsmanship and oak isn't light by any means. The man's size and strength are needed to move all the furniture every night. Cap looks back at him. His shaggy red hair shook when he laughed at something Logan said.

Tucking his t-shirt in, he walks over to the two men. They stop talking when he gets close, looking him over with less amusement. "That's much better," the barkeep says, with a thick accent like the two soldiers at the gate yesterday, "I hate to see a man embarrass himself after a night of drinking ale."

"Do I dare ask what happened last night?" Cap asks.

Logan just smiles, "You wanna tell him, John?"

John smiles as the memory of last night flooded in, "You seemed to think that it was your duty to challenge a couple of ladies to dice last night. You had no chance. You couldn't even stand up without help!" He chuckled as he said the last part.

Cap leans against the wall, thinking the world was going to end. After a few moments, he began to wish that it would. "So, now what?" he asks them.

Logan's face turns grave, "Well, I told the knights what happened.

They weren't too happy to hear the news. I can understand why. They're takin' it to the king. We're supposed to wait here till they're done."

John also adds, "I have a bad feeling about this. They have already added extra guards to the walls. There is also talk of asking for volunteers for a militia. Nothing good can come of this."

Cap forgets his hangover while listening, "But what's our part in all this."

"Not sure," Logan answers.

"The people believe that you are the prophecy come true," John adds, "If that is true, we have reason to fear. That only means that war is coming, and many innocent people will perish in-between the two sides."

"Prophecy," Cap states, "I remember hearing about this prophecy. But, what is it exactly?"

"We can show you," John tells him, "but, we won't be able to explain it."

Logan stands up, "Its Greek to me, but you might be able to understand it. Whether you are, or aren't, if you can figure at least a part of it out it could help us all."

"Well," Cap says, "It couldn't hurt. If I can help, at least I could make myself useful."

"We shouldn't be gone long," John says, "We can get back before the knights come for you two."

The three leave the tavern, John leaving the bar maids in charge. The three girls giggle as Cap walks by. He turns red with embarrassment as he looks back. The three men walk through the streets. People greet them almost cheerfully as they pass. Everyone has a smile upon their face, but there is nervousness in their voices. Cap can't help but feel the fear in the air. 'It feels so thick, you could cut it with a knife,' he thinks to himself. He thinks back to the fight with the zombies. They seemed to be easy enough to kill. A large amount seems fearful, but there seems to be enough soldiers within the walls to handle all the ones he and Logan seen. There must be something else that is frightening everyone.

The trio slows when they arrive into an open area. Cap can only describe it as the town square. Right there, against the backdrop of the castle's walls, stood a stockade and wooden post. Clear as day, nailed to the post was a piece of paper.

Logan points to it, "Well, there it is. Go take a look."

Cap looks at him with an almost unbelieving smile. He walks up to the parchment, and begins to read slow and carefully. After a minute or two, he turns to Logan and John, who are walking towards him. He looks back at it, and reads it out loud:

> "He comes from a land far away
> He will show after the quake
> With knowledge his weapon and history his shield
> He will bring change to our horrid ordeal
> During our greatest time of need
> He will fight for you and me
> In the land of Immortalis"

John asks Cap, "Well? What do you think?"

"It seems incomplete," Cap answers, "This could be anybody, with any result. It really feels like there should be more of an answer to this. The only two for sure things is that it's a male, and that he's going to be educated. This can be everyone and anyone. There really needs to be more than this for me to answer anything."

"What about showing after the quake?" John asks.

Cap looks at him quizzically, "How often does that happen?"

"Not often at all," John answers, "but lately, there have been more than what is normal."

"Earthquakes only happen when someone from our world arrives in Immortalis," Logan adds.

John nods his head in agreement, "There have gone times when it doesn't quake for hundreds of years. But this time, there were two quakes. Each less than a few hours apart."

"Two?" Cap asks, "But if I was one, who is the other?"

"We have no idea," John answers, "That's why we thought that you would be able to tell us."

They continue to discuss the prophecy, losing track of time. They stop talking as the sound of metal reaches their ears. Turning to see what the sound is, a knight clad in shining silver colored armor runs up to them. He is breathing hard, and Cap understands the feeling. The armor must be heavy, and the knight seems unaccustomed to running in it.

"You weren't where you were supposed to be," he says between breaths.

"Sorry, my liege," John says, "Logan and Cap are ready to see the king."

"Follow me, gentlemen," orders the knight. He turns around and walks along the wall, Cap and Logan following. He leads them to the main gate of the castle. The knight called something out to the guards above, then stands still, waiting for the gate to open. They stand in silence, as the two doors of the gate swung outward. The knight walks through, motioning for the two to follow. After they walk in, the gates close behind them, two guards locking the doors.

They walk through a dimly lit corridor, the masonry laid intricately. Designs along the walls were delicately carved into the stone. Cap is surprised that it doesn't smell damp, or feels that way either. It is warm and dry, the scent of roses filling the air. As they walk through the hallway, Cap could see doors on his left and right, at different intervals. They reach a door on the right, just before the hallway turns to the left.

The knight opens the door, "Wait here," he orders.

Cap and Logan walk into a brightly lit room. Torches surrounding the area were burning brightly. The stone ceiling's color is a light gray, with heavy oak rafters holding up the weight. The walls were painted a radiant red. The floors were recently swept revealing the stone bricks and mortar. Opposite where they're standing stood a large throne. Cap can't tell what it is made of, but the frame shined in the light, with the cushions a majestic purple. The throne sits higher than the rest of the room. The only other doors in the room, right behind the throne, were two gold plated doors, each one on separate walls. The walls spread outward from each of the doors, ending at the back wall.

Cap's understanding begins to comprehend the architecture. Everyone seated or standing in the room is almost forced to look at the person up front. The throne, being raised, made sure everyone looked up at the person sitting upon it. This must create the illusion of a commanding presence, whether it is wanted or not. Anyone in front would undoubtedly have the attention of the room. It is intelligent and magnificent at the same time. Cap can't help but smile. It just seems too good to be true.

Cap's study of the room is interrupted when the doors behind the throne are slammed open. He looks at the doors and watches as two knights walk in, and stand beside the throne.

Logan whispers to Cap, "These are Knights of the Round Table."

Cap just nods, confused. He takes a good look at the knights. They were all dressed in shiny armor, completely uniform. They looked the same from helmet to boots, including the shields. Then and there, it dawns on him. 'This is REAL!' Everything he knew as real no longer seems to apply anymore. As he realizes this, he can't help but feel sorrowful. Although, he is also excited at this brand new prospect entering into his life.

"Gentlemen, please, come with us," the knight on the left says. He walks through the doors, Cap and Logan following with the second knight right behind them. They enter a very small hallway, barely wide enough for a man to walk through. Unlike the other parts of the castle they've been through, this is very plain. No decorations are seen of any kind. It is very dusty, and very humid. Footprints are scattered all over the un-swept floor. The room isn't warm, but chilly. One can't help but feel cramped in the small area, and Cap can feel his breaths getting shorter the farther in they walk in the confined area. It is very dimly lit, with just enough light to see where to go, and that is it.

They come to a door at a dead end in the hallway, candles in candle holders on both sides. The knight in front of them twists the candle on the right. A noise is heard, creaking, then the sound of stones scraping against each other. To the left, the wall seems to open, showing another dimly lit passageway. As they walk through, a small boy waiting for them to pass holds a straw broom. 'It has to be for sweeping away the tracks,' Cap thinks to himself. As they walk on, the light grows brighter, but the hallway remains small and unchanged.

The group stops at a door on the right wall. As they enter this room, Cap notices that it is dismal compared to the previous room that they were in. This room has a plain chandelier hanging from the center of the rafters below the ceiling. The walls are but plain stone. No carvings, no anything of decoration, accept a list against the far wall. It's a large room though, and in its center is a large table. The Round Table. The knights close and bolt the door closes behind them, locking them in with only a door opposite them the only route out.

"And we wait again," Cap tells Logan.

"It won't be for long," Logan answers quietly.

He's right. The door opens suddenly, and knights begin to fill the room. Cap can only try to hide his enthusiasm. To be in the same room as the Knights of the Round Table is more than he could have ever dreamed of. He stands in awe as all the knights surround the table, the two who escorted them joining the larger group. Cap counts twenty-nine men in all. They stand in their perceived spots and wait, leaving only one spot open at the table. Who they are waiting for is soon answered.

Walking in silently, the king stands out from all the others. He is an older man, but not old. His hair is gray, but his eyes are still young, clear and bright. He has both energy and experience. He wears no helmet, just a small crown of gold. Except from the color, it is almost invisible upon his head. His armor is of silver, giving it a different shine than those of his knights. He walks to the open space at the table. Once there, all of them place their hands in front on the table, and begin speaking something that Cap can't understand. A much older man walks in silently as they spoke, and stands, waiting. He does look old, including his eyes. He has long gray hair, and a long untrimmed beard. His robe is a dark shade of gray. He is not a knight, obviously, but can only be an advisor of some sort.

When the knights finish speaking, they all sit down. All except for the old man, Logan, and Cap. The king nods silently to the man, and he walks over to Cap. Cap stands still, confused. The man stands directly in front of him, places his hands on each side of his face, closes his eyes, and begins to enchant something Cap can't understand. Cap begins to see bright colors circling around him. Fear begins to consume him at the sight. He feels a hand on his shoulder, but only sees the lights and can only hear the voice of the old man.

Only after what feels like hours, does the voice stop speaking. A few moments later, the lights begin to fade away. He stands there with a blank look on his face. The man in front of him looks into his eyes, his arms crossed in front of him. After a moment, nods his head in approval, then turns and walks behind the king. There he stands and waits.

The king stands up, "Can you hear me?"

"Very clearly, sir," Cap responds.

"Good. I am King Arthur Pendragon. The spell that Merlin has cast upon you gives you the ability to understand and speak all of the languages of the land. There are less complicated ways, but they can be demonic. There is no way of knowing how you could turn out if used.

"Now then, can you tell me how you arrived here? Not to Avalon, but to Immortalis."

Cap looks at the king, "No sir. I don't have any idea how I arrived here."

Merlin leans over and whispers something into the king's ear. The king nods and turns his attention back to Cap. "Tell me truthfully, were you being chased by someone?"

The bewildered look on Cap's face gave the king the answer before Cap could. "Well, yes. But how-"

The king interrupts, "Why was he after you?"

Cap's face turns from confused to grave, "I would rather not say."

"Do you know who he is?" the king asks.

"Yes," Cap answers.

The king wait's a moment for more, but Cap just stands there. "Will you tell us who it is then?" Cap just stands stone faced. King Arthur, seeing that this isn't getting him anywhere, looks at both men. "Gentlemen, tell me about what you saw."

Logan begins to tell the tale. He starts with finding Cap in the night, and the walk on the road. Cap tries to add pieces here and there, but it is Logan who's explaining with clarity. When, he gets to the part of the pterippus saving them, all of their listeners sit straight up, paying very close attention to what is being said. Logan ends the tale with their arrival to Avalon.

The knights whisper to each other for a few minutes, as Logan and Cap stand there. They keep their voices low, but even inaudible, they show worry. They finish talking amongst each other, and look towards the king.

He sits, staring at Cap. "Sir Percival, would you please see Mr. Logan back into town. The rest of you, check our readiness for battle. Mr. Cap, if you would come with me, please."

Everyone stands as the king gets out of his chair. Sir Percival walks behind Cap and Logan, and unlocks the door. He and Logan leave abruptly after. The rest of the knights leave through the opposite door. Cap waits as King Arthur stands, then follows him out the same door, Merlin behind them. They walk through a small archway, and up spiraling stairs, too many stairs in Cap's mind. They come out on a balcony near the top of the castle.

King Arthur goes to the edge and leans against the small guard wall. Cap slowly walks up and joins him. The king just stares at the lands around Avalon. Night has fallen, and the moon and stars give the land a ghostly, yet beautiful, appearance.

"I'm sure you have many questions, but I need you to answer mine first. They may seem and sound insignificant, yet Avalon and many lives, depend on what you say," the king tells Cap.

"Sire, it is a personal matter. I don't understand how someone chasing me would make such a difference in this land." he answers.

Merlin walks up to them, "Everything makes a difference in Immortalis, Mr. Cap."

Cap turns to him, "It is just Cap. I'm not a mister, and not a sir. I would greatly appreciate it if you just called me Cap."

King Arthur speaks into the night, "Cap, we must know. Why is this person chasing you?"

Cap sighs, "It was about a girl. We were both after the same girl, although neither of us knew it. Eventually, I found out about it. Instead of causing problems by continuing my pursuit, I backed off. I didn't let either of them know why I was becoming less and less available to them. He thought something was wrong, and she became worried.

"One night, she showed up unannounced to my home. She had only come to talk, and I was content with that. During the conversation, she broke down and began to cry. I went to console her. She began to cry into my shoulder, holding on to me tightly. That's when he walked in. Perception is everything, and he perceived that I stole the woman he loved. Nothing I could do or say would change his mind.

"Then, there came the day when he finally snapped. He followed me into the mountains. A trip I take every year. A forest fire had broken out. He took the opportunity for revenge. He tried to kill me and chased me into the burning trees. He wants me dead. He won't be happy until he gets his revenge."

King Arthur continues to gaze across the land. He nods his head in understanding, yet his face still shows confusion. Merlin steps back, lost among his own thoughts. King Arthur places his hand on Cap's shoulder. Cap hangs his head, ashamed and disappointed with reliving the events.

The king looks at the man beside him, and sees a tear fall in the moonlight. "Close your eyes, Cap," the king says, and waits as the young man obeys, "Now, tell me what you hear."

"The breeze, and off in the distance soft, but rolling thunder," Cap replies.

"And smell?"

"Flowers, grass, and…rain."

"Feel?"

"The breeze, but its colder. Much colder than the air around us."

Merlin walks back up, curious of the conversation.

King Arthur continues, "Now, look. Tell me what you see."

Cap opens his eyes, and stares across the land, "Rolling fields, the grass following in the breeze. Off in the distance, thunder clouds are building." Something catches his eye below. He tilts his head to see what it is and his eyes get wide open. Below them was walking the most beautiful woman he had ever seen in his life. She had long brown hair, and her body shimmers like silver in the moonlight. She was too far down to see any real features, but her beauty seems to radiate all around her. "And beauty, pure beauty."

The king looks where Cap is looking, and laughs "Beauty, yes, your eyes aren't deceiving you. Pure unadulterated beauty."

Merlin steps up, determined to get the conversation back on track. "Storms are uncommon in Immortalis, Cap. It can only mean that trouble is coming."

Cap turns to look at him, "Does this have to do with the prophecy?"

Merlin looks him in the eyes, "That depends on you."

"But it is not complete. I read it. There's nothing about that. It's way too open," Cap says.

"With good reason," the king says, "There's more. It has been separated into different places. This isn't heaven, Cap. There is still evil, and many that want to end our way of life."

Cap's frustration begins to show, "But that still doesn't answer anything! I'm no hero! I'm just a normal human who-"

"THERE!" the king shouts, pointing to something in the distance. Cap looks towards the area and sees a dark figure running towards Avalon.

As it gets closer, he can see that it is a wolf. A very large, black, wolf.

King Arthur turns and begins to run, "Quickly," he shouts, "We must get to the gate!"

They run through the castle, bursting through doors, and tearing through curtains. At times it seems that they are flying down stairways. Then it is through the castle gates and into town. Cap has no time to see where they are, or where they're headed. He can only concentrate on keeping up with the king. They continue to run, only stopping once they arrive at the town's gates.

"Let him enter!" King Arthur orders, startling the unsuspecting guards in front of him. They open the gates, but there's no wolf. Only a man gasping for air. He is very tall with dark, black hair. His clothing is made from wolves' fur. Fur that is just as black as his hair. He enters the town, and the gates close directly behind him. "My lord," he says between breaths when he sees the king.

The king's look is stern, "Adolf, my noble werewolf, please tell me you rush here with good news for me."

"Nay, my lord," he replies, "It is true, he has begun to amass his army. Hundreds have already been gathered."

"Is it she?"

"Yes, she and most of her clan."

The king motions for one of the soldiers nearby, "Double the guards. Get everyone on alert. Make sure the path out of town is clear! Go, now!"

"There's more," Adolf says, "They have found a man. He is hateful, and wants vengeance. His only ambition is to kill one man."

Cap swallows hard, "Who?"

"You," Adolf answers.

Cap's face turns grave. King Arthur seems to take no notice. He grabs Cap by the shoulders, shaking him slightly. "Tell me, who followed you?" Cap remains speechless, just staring into the void of night. "Tell me Cap! He's going to use this man's vengeance for you to destroy all of Immortalis. He'll do it knowing he only wants to kill you! Now tell me!"

Cap lowers his head in shame, "His name is Luke. My brother."

Chapter 4

Luke wakes in fear. What happened feels like a nightmare. He didn't wake under the tree, but in a cave. From where he lays he can see a red light on the ceiling above, hanging high from a stalactite. He is covered with a blanket of black fur. He throws the blanket off and sits up, leaning against the wall of the cave. He notices two different types of creatures moving around the cave.

'Disgusting little things,' he thinks. The tall beings look like people, except their skin is a pale green, clothes are tattered and torn, and their hands and feet look like claws. Their freakish appearance begins to turn his stomach, so he turns his attention to the smaller creatures. They are much shorter, a little larger than a child. They seem to be well clothed, but what style, Luke can not distinguish. They have small, but well proportioned wings on their back. They're arms and heads are covered in short reddish-brown fur. Humanoids, yet nothing like humans. They seem to be in control of the taller things. They give orders, but in a language he can not comprehend.

Movement to the right catches his eye. From a separate entrance opposite the main of the cave, a beautiful woman walks towards him. She's not tall, about five feet, maybe an inch or two more. Her long blonde hair is braided all the way down to her thighs. Her dress is white, and shows her thin figure very well. The fur coat upon her back is a dark grey. She walks very gracefully, like a cat. Her smile shows warmth, but her green eyes look cold. In her hands, she is carrying a golden cup.

Kneeling down to him, she hands him the cup. She says something to him in a language that sounds like French. He shakes his head with a very confused look on his face. She smiles and makes a motion for him to drink. Looking at the liquid, he sees red with purple streaks and swirls. It smells bitter and he pushes the cup away from his face, reluctant to drink it. She melts away his reluctance with another warm smile. He lifts the cup, and drinks.

He is so thirsty, he doesn't taste it at first. Bitterness suddenly touches his tongue, and then…blood? Her smile turns cold as she helps him by tilting the cup as he downs the drink, forcing every last drop into his throat. He swallows the last drop, and then drops the cup as the world goes white, then a loud "*pop*" in his ears. Colors and the world come back into view, and he can suddenly understand what the little people are saying to the ugly tall things.

"That's better," the woman says, getting his attention. He couldn't help but think that her voice sounds as sweet as honey. "Can you understand me now?" He nods his head yes, but continues to look very confused.

"Where am I? Who are you?" he asks.

"I am Martine," she answers, "You are in a land that is not your own. You have been brought here for a very *special* reason."

"And what's that?" he inquires.

She smiles coldly, "To kill the man you followed here."

Luke smiles, "Happily. Just take me to him."

A man's voice comes from within the cave, "It is not that easy." Martine stands and walks backwards to the opposite wall as the voice speaks. "For me to give you your vengeance, you must give me mine."

"I don't make deals with someone I can't see," Luke states confidently into the air. He hears a small chuckle echo throughout the cave. In walks a tall man. He has blonde-brownish hair, and a neatly trimmed beard. The tall and small things all stop moving around and bow as he walks over to an outcropping of rocks. He suddenly appears larger than the cave as he turns and sits on the rocks. The outcropping now looking like a large throne with the man's increased size.

"And I," he says looking at Luke, "don't make any deal with a mortal I don't know the name of."

"My name is Luke," he says proudly, "and who are you?"

The man smiles, and looks at one of the small things, "Salma, get the imps and zombies out of here," he turns back to Luke after the imps and zombies are gone, "I am the titan Cronus, father of the gods," he tells him.

Luke's face shows signs of disbelief, "That's not possible. That's mythology. Its fiction, nothing more than a child's story."

"I AM Cronus!" he bellows, the sound throwing Luke against the wall. "I created this land when I was banished from my own."

"H-how?" stammers Luke with fear.

Cronus turns to Martine, "Martine, go get the others while I explain to this mortal about our world." She bows, and leaves into the inner cave.

Cronus turns his attention back to Luke, "I created this land in my own vision. This land is a safe haven from non-believers and persecutors. My mistake was that I wasn't *more* specific in my rules of the land. Now, all beings and creatures of ancient or no longer existent beliefs reside here. Mortals who believed, or refused to convert to the new beliefs of the time, also reside here.

"Because of this, the land has been split by an ancient feud between my son, Zeus, and I. I'm in control of the western lands and mountains, and he the eastern. These many millennia have done nothing to calm my anger, and I still resent being cast out of my own home.

"With more and more mythical and mortal creatures that have arrived in between the beginning and now, I have been able to build a force that's lethal enough to invade his lands. You'll be the one to take my army to the eastern mountains."

"Me?" Luke questions, "But you're a titan. You are much more powerful than me. How could I be better than you?"

Cronus smiles at the question, "The battle between gods and titans should be between gods and titans. My son has his own forces built. I need a mortal's touch to open the path for me. I promise you, you will get your revenge, but only if I get mine. If you kill your man before my own vengeance, my vengeance will be on you. Understood?"

The two were so concentrated in their conversation that Luke doesn't notice that others are now standing around them. Luke takes a little time to think as he looks around. "And I will be able to get my revenge how I want it?" He smiles evilly, "Cronus, we have a deal."

Cronus' smile illuminates the cave, "Good, now let's meet your fellow commanders," he points to Martine, "You've already met Martine. She and her werecat pride are an invaluable source. You will find them most useful when the time comes."

He then points to a tall, voluptuous woman. Her long dark hair brings out her pale skin and bright blue eyes. Her black dress shows every curve, and a black cape that seems to float in the air around her ankles. The look on her face was of disappointment, but no other emotion shows, "My second in command, this is Breanna. Her vampire clan is indispensable to my plans of invasion."

He then points to the imp he had spoken to before, "Salma, leader of the imps. It is the imps' magic that allows us to control our zombie army.

"Now, on to business. Breanna, Salma has the zombies ready for movement. You two will attack Avalon. Sack Avalon by any means necessary. We need the river to further our progress eastward.

"Luke, you will go and retrieve the Leviathan from the north mountain lake."

Luke protests, "But I thought you wanted me to lead the army?"

Cronus' face gets stern, "You WILL retrieve the Leviathan! Your time will come soon enough. Martine, you and your pride will take him there. Make sure he stays alive."

"We will, sire," she answers him.

Breanna walks over to Cronus, speaking just loud enough that only he can hear her, "This doesn't seem right, using the mortal to destroy everything in his way for revenge."

Cronus speaks back in the same volume, "If they're prophecy is true, Breanna, this is the only way we will be victorious. We've discussed this possibility many times."

"I know, sire," she says, "but that doesn't change how it all seems dishonorable."

Cronus smiles at her, and then speaks loud enough for all to hear, "Victory by any means possible. We've waited too long to be thwarted by anything. Only death awaits surrender, and our victory will bring much honor. Avalon and the Leviathan first. We will discuss the rest afterwards." He stands abruptly, walking to the inner cave. His body goes back to its smaller human form as he walks into it. The four commanders are left to their own thoughts.

Martine gets a mischievous grin on her face, "Issues, Breanna?"

"Shut it Martine," Breanna orders.

Luke laughs, "Such fire. Let me lay the blanket down. I can work that out of you." She looks at him, her blue eyes cold as ice. He sees movement, then the feeling of being thrown. He finds himself suspended in the air against the wall. Breanna's hand is around his throat.

Her blue eyes show instant death as she speaks to Luke, "Listen! You insolent, puny, mortal! It would be nothing for me to bite you and take you under my control. But I think death would be a better fit. You would make a better zombie. Worthless human!" her hand begins to squeeze tighter, and Luke's face begins to turn purple.

Salma speaks to her in calm, soothing voice, "Madam, we have preparations to make."

Breanna drops Luke to the floor, "Time to do your job, Martine. Get him the hell out of here before *I* kill him," and she was gone. She is nowhere to be seen. Salma bows to Martine, and flies out of the main entrance of the cave. Martine walks to Luke, helping him to his feet.

"She likes me," he says hoarsely, holding his throat. They both laugh as she leads him inward.

Chapter 5

Dawn brings its light upon the land. King Arthur, Adolf, and Cap look over the land on the castle balcony. Each one is silent, lost in thoughts of battle and impending danger. Fingers of light reach the western horizon. There, among the first rays of light, stand the lines of hundreds of zombies, their pale green skin reflecting its sick color from the sun.

"So it begins," King Arthur says with disappointment. Adolf and Cap nod their heads in silent agreement. They continue watching, waiting to see what will happen next.

A young boy comes running onto the balcony, "My lord, the Army has arrived!"

"Thank you, son. Go spread the message. Let everyone know to be ready," the king tells him.

"Yes, sire," the boy says, and runs out.

King Arthur turns around, his face very pale. "I must get ready for battle."

"Sire, do you think that is wise?" Cap asks.

King Arthur looks at Cap with sorrow, "These are my people. I must protect them at all costs."

"Only," Adolf adds, "they won't attack until she's able to command. They will wait till nightfall, or till the clouds block the sky."

Cap looks back at the western sky. The thunderclouds are still building there, but still very far off. Unless they picked up speed, they won't arrive until close to dusk. "Who is this "She"?" he asks.

"Breanna, clan leader of the vampires and his second in charge." Adolf answers.

"She's a vampire also?" Cap asks.

"Of course," Adolf says, "The most powerful of them all."

An idea begins to form in Cap's head, "And my brother will be with her?"

The king looks at him curiously, "Probably. His only goal in life is revenge. I would expect him to be here."

"What's the name of the next town?" Cap asks.

"El Dorado," King Arthur answers with a curious look on his face.

The wheels in Cap's head begin to turn faster, "How long would it take to get to the next town?"

Adolf now looks hat him curiously, "About a day. What are you thinking of?"

Cap smiles, "Wait a second." he tells Adolf. Turning to King Arthur, he asks, "Your highness, what will you need to do to get the rest of the land notified and ready?"

"I would need messengers to run from town to town, to alert the land. I would need to get to the City of Caesars to speak with the council. Most of all, New Olympus must be notified immediately." the king answers him, "I'm curious also, Cap. What are you planning?"

"Look," Cap says pointing to the army, "they aren't moving."

"Of course," says Adolf, "They will wait for her. I've already mentioned that."

"I don't think they are planning a long siege," Cap points out.

"What are you talking about?" asks King Arthur, "We need to attack them before they attack us. We must reduce their forces before nightfall."

"I don't think so," Cap smiles at the thought that has formed in his head, "If you attack now, you chance dwindling your own forces, making Avalon more vulnerable when darkness does fall upon us."

The king's face shows that he is beginning to understand, but not quite, "What would you have us do?"

"You need to leave for the City of Caesars right away. Have your knights escort the townspeople to El Dorado. Dispatch messengers immediately to all the other towns." Cap says confidently.

"And you?" Adolf asks.

"I'll stay and fight," Cap answers

King Arthur protests, "But, if you are the prophecy, we will need you alive."

"Do they know about this 'prophecy'?" Cap asks.

"Yes," answers the king, "I would presume that is why they are attacking now."

"Then I need to stay," Cap says, "They're using my brother against me and all of you. The army won't leave here till I'm captured or dead. My brother is stubborn. He won't let me leave here alive. If I'm sacrificed, my brother won't be able to hurt anyone any more. His need for revenge will be filled, and you'll have more time to get forces together to battle this army."

Adolf's face is full of curiosity, "You're going to sacrifice yourself, and Avalon? You're insane!"

"Maybe, but it fits," Cap says, "If we all stay, there's a chance that we all die. No one else would know that the army is coming or what happened here."

King Arthur nods his head in agreement, "I see your point. I'll send armed escorts with the townsmen. My knights will take over command."

"No," Cap demands.

King Arthur looks at him sternly, "What?"

Cap looks the king in the eye, "Relinquish command of Avalon to me. I've heard its part of the Code of Chivalry to protect the weak and helpless. Send the knights with the townspeople. Take a couple with you also. Leave me with as many men as you can spare, and all that might volunteer. Your knights are great warriors. They will be needed in a much larger battle than this one. We'll try to hold them off till daylight. That should be sufficient time for everyone to get to safety."

"Alright," King Arthur says reluctantly, "I don't like it, but I cannot find an argument against it," he turns, and calls inside the castle, "Sir Dagonet, let everyone know that Cap is taking command of Avalon. You, Sir Lancelot, and Sir Gawain will accompany me to the City of Caesars. Have Sir Palamedes take command of the knights and escort the people of Avalon to El Dorado. All other volunteers will be appreciated to stay."

"Right away sir," he says, and leaves abruptly.

King Arthur turns back to Cap, "What else will you need?"

Cap smiles again, "A weapon and men ready to fight."

"I'll stay," says Adolf.

"As will I," says Merlin, appearing out of nowhere.

"It is a start," says the king smiling, "Let's go to the armory." They leave the balcony. They walk through the castle to a colder, darker area. It is dismal in light and appearance. The room in front of them is guarded by two soldiers. They move to the side, saluting as King Arthur and his three companions walk into the room. Cap can't believe his eyes at the amount of weapons in this room. There are weapons from almost every era in history. The weapons range from axes to the xiphos, and every weapon of human destruction in between.

"Which one catches your eye?" King Arthur asks.

"I don't know. A gun would be nice, but I don't see one," Cap answers.

"Here," King Arthur tells him, "guns are considered dishonorable."

Cap doesn't understand. Logan has one. "Since when does honor have anything to do with winning a battle?" he mumbles under his breath. He doesn't argue though. He looks at each weapon, thinking of what each one can do. He sees one that catches his eye. It is much different than any of the others. It's very shiny, but orange in color. At the top is a mace that's attached to a long rod that goes down about four feet, then curves into another rod about two feet long, a sharp spike at its end. Cap grabs it, testing its weight and balance. He twirls, spins, and swings it around. He can't help but feel that it is both natural and comfortable.

"What is this one?" he asks.

King Arthur smiles at him, "That is the Exitialis Arma."

"I like it," Cap says, "I'll take this one."

"As you wish," the king tells him, "Now it is our tradition to name our weapons. What would you like to name yours?"

Cap looks at the weapon in his hands. He thinks back to his childhood, then to his adulthood. Only one name seems to stand out among all the memories. "Adflictus," he says, "I wish to call it Adflictus."

King Arthur, Merlin, and Adolf all look on with approval. It sounds like a very good name. King Arthur pulls out Excalibur, "Kneel Cap." Cap looks very confused, but obeys. "Give me your full name."

"Casey Cenere," he says.

The king taps each of his shoulders and says, "Now rise, Sir Casey, Commander of Avalon."

Cap stands up, "Thank you, sire. I would still like to be called Cap though."

"If you would like," King Arthur says, "Now you have the title and the command."

Cap smiles, "I guess I can't get mad about being called 'sir' anymore."

Adolf chuckles, "No, sir."

Merlin's face remains like stone, "We need to get you out of here, sire."

"Yes," the king says sadly, "I need to be off." They leave the room and the castle. Walking through the streets, silent but aware. As they get closer to the back gate, they couldn't help but notice the fear in the townspeople's eyes as they grabbed their belongings. They are reluctant to go, and yet, ready to be gone. It touches the group's hearts in a way that cannot be explained. They remain poised and steadfast. Although, they feel sorry for the people, and fearful for those that choose to remain behind.

Sir Dagonet, Sir Gawain, and Sir Lancelot are waiting for the king at the gate when they arrive. They can here Sir Palomedes issuing orders to the knights and townspeople behind them. The three knights have a white horse waiting, along with three brown ones for themselves. Cap, Adolf, and Merlin wait as they climb upon the horses' backs.

"Well," Cap says, "I wish you best of luck on your journey. I'd like to say see you later, but farewell is a better fit. It was an honor to meet you, King Arthur."

The king looks back at him, "The honor is mine. Farewell, Sir Casey."

Cap yells at the gate's guards, "Open the gates. Let everyone out. Close them immediately afterwards. Let no one in." As the gates open he turns to his two companions, "Let's go."

Adolf smiles, "Of course, Sir Casey." Cap just growls, but doesn't say a word as they all walk away.

King Arthur smiles, and then laughs as he turns his horse and rides out with his three knights. He begins laughing softly, confusing his three knights.

"Sire," one of the knights speaks, "May I ask why you're so merry?"

"Don't you see it, Sir Gawain?" the king replies, "He is the prophecy come true."

"How do you know?" Sir Gawain asks.

King Arthur turns around in his saddle, "Sir Lancelot, would you please entertain part of our journey by reciting the prophecy for us?"

Sir Lancelot clears his throat, and speaks loud and clear to his three companions in front of him:

"He comes from a land far away
He will show after the quake
With knowledge his weapon and history his shield
He will bring change to our horrid ordeal
During our greatest time of need
He will fight for you and me
In the land of Immortalis.

With free thought and freedom he will march alone
Finding friends on the way, making many foes
He will see our good, and learn their evil
He'll be forced to fight, and blood will be spilt
But he will march on, against all odds
Unwavering into the Kingdom of Gods
In the land of Immortalis.

Here he will live, here it will begin
The war we've been fighting will come to an end
Because he will make the greatest sacrifice
We will once again be able to thrive
Through many pains, he'll fight for us to be free
From the demons and monsters that want us in slavery

Here in the land of Immortalis."

Chapter 6

Cap stands on the ramparts of the city wall, looking at the army that has moved closer, along with the thunderstorm above them. They have stopped a few hundred yards away from the wall. Apparently, they're waiting for their commander's orders. He looks upon the walls. Sentries are placed strategically in intervals. Lightning flashes and thunder is heard from the distance. It is almost time.

Cap turns to Adolf and asks, "You've had most of the men rest?"

"Yes sir," Adolf answers.

"You better have someone wake the rest of them. We'll need all of the men at their stations."

Adolf calls a man over and sends him off. He turns back to Cap, "I've also asked for volunteers from the dungeon. All have offered services."

Cap smiles, "That's good. We're gonna need all the help we can get. I have one more idea, though. Have every torch, lamp, and light of any kind lit. I have a feeling once it gets dark, those lights will be our only advantage. We should have some men go do that now."

Adolf leaves to give out his orders. Cap's heart is starting to beat faster with anticipation and fear. He leans against Adflictus, trying to appear calm. He doesn't want to show fear in front of the men. He cannot show fear. He can feel the eyes of the men upon him. Unsure, and yet relying on his command to get them through this. The added pressure doesn't help his anticipation in any way.

Adolf walks back up to him. He walks with quiet assuredness, but his face shows worry. Cap looks over at him, "Tell me something. Were you the wolf I seen running to the town last night?"

Adolf smiles, "I am."

Cap looks at him incredulously, "You can't be!"

Adolf laughs, "I am a werewolf. I drank a potion to understand the languages, instead of Merlin's spell. I've never been one to trust in magic. It took less time, and was far simpler. It had its side effects though. This is what I have become because of it."

"So, you could probably slip out of town undetected? Maybe, get behind their lines?" Cap asks.

"Yes, I could," Adolf answers him, "But you would be one man less."

Cap looks at him with confidence, "And you would be free to move, and cause damage behind their lines." Cap's silent for a moment, "Do that. If they think they are being attacked from the front and rear, it may give us a little more time."

"Yes sir!" Adolf says excitedly. He turns and walks away quickly.

Cap calls out to him, "Be careful. Don't take too many unnecessary chances." Adolf doesn't look back. He waves a hand in the air and continues walking.

Cap looks at the sky. The clouds are almost upon them, and it's beginning to get dark. He looks across the field at the army, and sees figures floating above them. The vampires have arrived. One is more noticeable than the rest. He looks directly at the figure and says, "Your move."

Across the field, Breanna floats above the zombie army, studying the situation. Something doesn't feel right. They've attempted smaller attacks on Avalon before, but the enemy's forces have always attacked before nightfall. This time they didn't attack at all. As she looks at the town lights begin to turn on. One by one, the city slowly illuminates. She throws out her heightened senses, learning about the men inside the walls. She can sense the fear of the men in the town, but one is different. He fears, but is also anxious, and excited. He could be very dangerous. She studies the lights again. As every window in the castle lights up, she sees a lone man standing along the city wall.

Her vision is exceptional, but she's questioning it now. That man looks a lot like Luke. Not exactly, but close enough to be his brother. This confuses her. She sends out all her senses, trying to learn who this man is. They reach him, and rush back to her. It is he. His fear, excitement, and anxiousness are all there, but more also. She can feel his need to protect, and a reluctance to fight. Yet, he is poised and ready also. Sadness, of all his feelings, sadness shows the most. She can feel his eyes gazing out upon the army, and it feels like he's looking at her.

She looks over her shoulder and yells, "Salma!" The imp flies up to her, "I want you and two other zombies to walk with me up to the city. I want a word with their commander, and a closer look at their defenses."

"Yes, Madam," Salma says, and then flies towards the backlines.

Breanna looks back at the town one more time. 'They have something planned. They have to be up to something.' she thinks. She looks over her army. It is larger than any they have ever massed before. They're nothing more than slaves, with imps and vampires controlling their actions. Of her vampires, she's worried many won't make it through tonight. She was hoping that Avalon would have attacked the zombies before nightfall, losing many of their soldiers in the process. That would have made it safer for her vampires tonight. She sighs as she floats to the ground, and walks over to Salma and the two zombies.

Lightning begins to flash quicker, and the thunder is getting louder as she gets to Salma. "It is dark enough. Let us go meet the enemy," she says. The group walks out onto the field.

Cap sees the four walking out before the soldier running up to him says anything. "Sir Casey!"

"I see them," Cap says. He walks down the staircase and over to the front gate. Merlin is at the gate waiting for him.

"She's getting closer to scout Avalon," he says.

Cap nods, "Then let's meet her out there so she doesn't get to close." He points to the guards, "Let us out. Close the gates behind us. Keep everyone down and out of sight till we get back."

The guards obey, opening the gate just enough to let them through. He and Merlin walk out without looking back. They can hear the gates close behind them. They walk quickly to intercept the four before they get too close to Avalon. As they get closer, he can start to see the features of the zombies, then the vampire and the little creature beside her. The wind picks up, and it begins to rain lightly as the two groups meet.

Cap looks them over, then into the eyes of the woman, "Ma'am, can we help you?"

She smiles coldly, "Surrender."

"No," Cap says.

"Many will die," Salma says.

"On both sides. We're prepared for death. Are you?" replies Cap.

"Terms of surrender then," Breanna says.

"Sure," Cap says smiling, "You surrender and I'll send your army home."

Breanna's anger begins to build, having to negotiate with a mere mortal, "YOU," she points at him, "You surrender. We will allow you and your men to live. You can be our pets and slaves. We might consider letting those not fighting to go free." She smiles triumphantly.

Cap continues smiling, and then laughs, "You can piss off if you think I'll surrender anyone to be a slave."

Breanna cannot control her anger any longer. "Mortal!" she yells. She's about to attack Cap, but the spike of his weapon is suddenly at her chin. For a moment Breanna thinks of killing him, but his eyes are deathly cold, and his hands are steady. His smile has faded to a determined crease on his face.

"Listen!" Cap yells, "I don't know who the hell you think you are. Do NOT expect me to be afraid of you. I know what you are, and I know what you're capable of. If you want to impress me, walk off of this field and take your army back from the hell you came from!"

Breanna's anger is fading a little bit, but her curiosity is peaked. "Who are you?" she asks.

Cap speaks, not moving his eyes or his weapon, "I am Cap, Commander of the forces of Avalon. I am the one Luke seeks, and I will not surrender this town without a fight. You know who I am. Now, who the hell are you two?"

"I am Breanna," she says, "Commander of the armies before you. This is the imp commander, Salma."

Cap lowers Adflictus to the ground very slowly, but ready to raise it at any moment. "Now, Breanna and Salma, you and I have walked out here in peace, we will walk away in peace. Unless you have anything else to add, we're done here. I need to get back to my men, and get ready for battle."

Breanna's eyes remain angry, but her voice is calm, "It would be in your best interest to surrender." The wind shifts directions as the rain falls harder. The scent of wet dog enters Cap's nostrils. Breanna smells it also. Her eyes change from angry to fearful.

Cap smiles. "Talk to me again in a couple of hours," he says. He and Merlin turn and walk away.

"That was brazen," Merlin says.

"Show no fear," Cap says smiling, "and always keep your guard up. When they attack, we will have the archers concentrate on the vampires only. I don't want any arrows, or ammunition of any kind wasted on the zombies."

Logan remains silently hidden in the bushes. He is amazed, and also proud of Cap for standing up to the much more superior being. He continues to watch the group in front of him. They stand there, silent and still.

Movement beside him startles him. A large wolf crouches beside him, eyeing the same group. "Damn it, Adolf," Logan whispers softly, "I've told you never to do that." He turns his attention back to the group.

Breanna looks down at her companion, "We're going to have a hell of a time with this one, Salma."

Salma looks up at her, "He's smart, he isn't going to be defeated easily. I am afraid that he will recognize our weaknesses, and use them to his advantage."

Breanna nods her head in agreement, "I need to kill him tonight. His courage deserves more than the murder Cronus will allow Luke to do."

Salma watches as Cap and Merlin enter the opening gates, speaking only when they are closed. "I wish you the best of luck. This one's not going to be killed easily." Breanna doesn't say anything. She just turns around, walking back to her army. Salma follows obediently.

Logan nudges Adolf. "I don't know what you have planned, but you better get moving. I'll stay here. I gotta a feeling I'll be in a good place to help." he whispers. Adolf doesn't make a sound. He backs off into the night, and disappears in the darkness.

Breanna waves her vampires and the imps over to her in front of the zombies. She remains silent until all of them circle her. "Send the zombies in first," she orders, "Let them waste all their ammunition and energy on the slaves first. When they are worn out, we'll attack with aggression. Be sure of your targets. This man, this Cap, he is intelligent, and will use any mistake to his advantage. Do not be careless! No one kills this Cap but me. Understand?" She waits until she sees them all nod in agreement. "Good. Now, on my word, we attack."

They all agree; nodding with respect, then leave to their stations. Breanna raises her arms and floats above her army. She turns toward Avalon and speaks, very softly to herself, "Alright, insolent mortal. Let us see if you're ready."

Cap watches as Breanna floats above the army. He turns to his soldiers, "Be ready! Here they come!" he yells. He looks back at Breanna. He can see her point towards the town and say something. His body tenses up, ready for action as the zombies begin to move forward.

"Wait till they get to the wall!" he yells, "Make the zombies work. Save your energy and ammunition for the vampires." He sees his archers tensing up, waiting for him to give the word. The soldiers along the wall are poised and ready for the zombies to climb up. Large rocks and their weapons are close at hand. Cap looks down at the soldiers on the ground behind him. They are also ready for battle, knowing the army will eventually get through the gates, or over the wall. Cap can't help but smile at the sight. Every soldier volunteered to stay, risking their lives to protect their family and friends. They should all be knighted for their bravery and sacrifice.

A zombie's shriek forces him to turn around. The zombies begin running toward the city walls. Out of the corner of his eye he sees a soldier grab a rock, pulling his arm back to throw it. "Wait!" he commands. He notices all the soldiers along the wall grabbing rocks as well. "Wait!" he commands again. The zombies reach the wall sooner than he anticipated. He raises Adflictus as he watches them scramble around. He keeps it held up. The zombies begin to crawl on each other, creating makeshift ladders out of themselves.

"Now!" Cap yells, dropping Adflictus quickly to his side. The rocks start showering down upon the dead beings. Shrieks and screams are heard from the dead and dying creatures. Cap nods to an archer, who lights the tip of his arrow on fire. He shoots it behind the army. A large flame blazes up entrapping the zombies between the wall with deadly thrown rocks, and a large wall of flame. 'Good God I love fire!' Cap thinks to himself. He looks back at the vampires across the field. "Next!" he yells into the night.

Breanna remains floating in the air, shocked. She looks on with anger and admiration as the word reaches her ears. She expected the zombies to take great losses, but she also expected them to penetrate the walls more quickly. This Cap is far more formidable than she suspected. She's not sure how to proceed though. The zombies will penetrate, but if she waits too long the danger of the sun can, and will, become a factor. If she moves in now, the losses for the vampires will be much higher. She must have the city though. She remembers what Cronus said, 'By any means necessary.' She looks around at her vampires, "Forward!" she commands, and then begins to fly slowly to battle. "Here we come," she says softly.

Adolf grins in the darkness as they fly off. His black wolf form perfectly camouflaging him into the dark night. He smiles with pride. 'Cap has her confused,' he thinks. He holds down a chuckle at the thought. He turns his attention back to his prey. The imps remain behind, using their magic to control their slaves. He only needs to confuse them to wreak havoc for their forces to get disoriented. He's about to jump out when he notices something. There is one imp that isn't concentrating on the battle, but giving orders to the other imps. He changes his mind about what he is going do immediately. He's going to capture the one in charge.

Meanwhile, Cap watches the vampires flying slowly towards him.

He raises Adflictus, his archers raising their bows at the sight. He waits till the flying force gets just close enough. Lightning flashes, the thunder crashes, and Cap drops his weapon to his side. Arrows fly through the wind and rain at the vampires. A few vampires fall with agonizing cries. Then they begin to fly faster. Cap readies for the fight when he hears a gunshot through the wind and thunder. Another vampire falls. He can see Breanna's face as she dodges arrows. It is full of worry. He hears odd sounds below, and looks down to see the zombies running around confused. In the distance he hears a wolf howl.

Cap looks back up to see the vampires upon them. "Let's go!" He yells. A vampire flies at him, and Cap swings the mace of Adlfictus into the chest of the creature, knocking it away from him. He flips Adflictus, throwing the spike into another vampire's temple. It falls dead to the ground. He looks around quickly to see all his soldiers in combat.

The zombies regroup, with no more attempts from the wall to stop them. Cap can see they are successfully climbing the wall without any interference. He looks up in time to dodge another attack from the closest vampire. It comes back after him. He ducks and swings Adflictus, catching the vampire through the leg with the spike. The vampire screams in agony. Cap spins around, tearing the vampires muscle, throwing it into a group of zombies. All of them fall to the ground. He turns around to see a hand come over the wall and drag a soldier to the ground. "Fall back!" he orders, jumping off the wall.

His troops follow suit. They enlarge the ground force that's been fighting attacking vampires, waiting for this moment to occur. Suddenly, the gates break, releasing the zombies into the town. His force is attacked from the air at the same time. The fighting becomes very fierce and relentless as his group of men is attacked from all sides. Cries of agony and pain can be heard coming from both forces.

Cap is using Adlfictus with all his strength. Blocking, striking, and dodging both vampires and zombies. He looks back at the broken gate in time to see Logan jump through the wall of fire. The old man fires off a shot, bringing a vampire to the ground. The opposing force is surprised, stunned for a moment from the rear attack, allowing Logan to join Cap's forces without incident.

"Thought you could use some help," Logan says.

"Glad to have you," Cap says. "Fall back! Fall back!" he orders behind him.

The group backs up, moving toward the back gate, slowly. They continue to fight off the opposing force, but seem to be losing more and more men by the minute. They continue to move and fight. Cap can't help but wonder if the morning is almost upon them, or if it will show at all.

Breanna waits floating behind her army, watching Cap. She's waiting for just the right opening to grab him. Then it is there. The enemy force is almost at the back gate. Just as she starts moving she hears Cap yell, "Let fly!" and arrows begin to fly over the back wall. Cap raises his weapon just in time to block Breanna's attack. She hits him with all her strength and speed as her vampires cry out in pain. Cap flies into an alleyway, his weapon landing a few feet away from him. He stands slowly, exhausted and hurting from the hit.

Breanna stands in front of him. "Surrender," she says.

Cap stands up straight, looking her in the eye, "No."

She smiles with cold eyes, "Then you die." She rushes towards him.

Cap gets hit again from his right as she moves, knocking him towards Adlfictus. He grabs it and gets up quickly. He turns ready to fight. Breanna's teeth are latched into the arm of the man who pushed him out of the way. The man is average height, with light brown hair. Cap's never seen him before, but he still looks familiar. The stranger struggles with Breanna then throws her off. He falls to his knees as the vampire's venom begins to affect him. Cap moves quickly to help him.

Breanna flies back, stops and floats in the air. "Diamondback!" she yells, and flies with tremendous speed to kill the man. Cap swings Adflictus over his head instinctively. The mace hits her in the back, knocking her down to the ground and stopping her progress. She winces with pain, and rolls over, and lies perfectly still. The point of Cap's weapon is right over her heart, his foot upon it.

The man gets up, suddenly unaffected by the bite. "Yes, Breanna, it's me," he says. "Now would be a good time to surrender."

Her face is full of hatred, "I'll have you all killed!" She tries to use her speed to move, but can't go anywhere.

Merlin walks up to her, his hand over her head, "Not today," his other hand is raised into the air, creating an invisible shield that will not allow her vampires that have left the battle to assist her. The zombies, also, have left the battle, attempting to assist their commander. The soldiers outside the area have taken the opportunity to attack the opposing force without any opposition fighting back.

Adolf walks up, holding the imp Salma, "I say we kill them both."

Breanna looks at Cap. His face is stern, his hands steady, and he is poised to kill. Almost exactly the same as when they met earlier tonight. His eyes aren't quite cold though. They show something else. Was it pity?

"What are your orders?" Cap asks. Breanna remains silent, turning her face away from him. "I'm only going to ask one more time. What are your orders?" She remains silent. His foot presses down on the spike, just enough to penetrate her skin. Just enough pressure for her to feel the pain. She looks at Cap with hatred filled eyes.

"Breanna!" Salma cries out.

She doesn't look away from Cap's eyes, "My orders. To take Avalon by any means necessary."

Light begins to show in the east. Cap smiles, mission accomplished. "Then here are our terms. You will call off your army. You will let my men, and myself, leave without incident. In return, you, Salma and your army are allowed to keep your lives. Do we have a deal?"

Breanna remains silent. To make the deal would be admitting defeat, but Avalon would be captured. To deny it would mean her life, Salma's, and her vampires with the chance of not acquiring the town. To live is the obvious choice, but to admit defeat isn't in her.

The man called Diamondback speaks up, "Kill them both. It would be two less commanders in their army."

Salma cries out to her with fear, "Breanna! Do it!" Cap's foot presses a little more on the spike.

Breanna looks at Cap. "Deal," she says ashamed.

Cap lifts his foot, and pulls Adflictus away from her. He nods his head to Adolf and Merlin. Adolf let's go of Salma and Merlin releases his magic, allowing Breanna to move. Salma runs to her to help.

"When you're ready," Cap says. Breanna nods her head yes, "Ok. Merlin let them go."

Merlin lowers his hand, his magical shield now gone. Breanna and Salma fly off to the west immediately, the vampires and zombies following. Cap feels bad for them, but joyous as well. He wasn't supposed to make it out alive. Though he knows how they feel about the loss, he looks around happy. Very few of his men have made it.

He looks at the man who saved his life, "Thank you."

"No problem," the man says. He holds out his hand for Cap to shake, "I'm Diamondback."

Cap grabs his hand and shakes it. "Cap," he says, "We need to talk."

Diamondback frowns at him, "You should have killed them. They get Avalon now."

"Yes, but we don't have the force to defend it again," Cap tells him.

Adolf smiles proudly, "Let's talk about this on the road. We only have a day to get out of here."

Cap agrees, "Yeah." He starts walking to the back gate. "Let's get moving to El Dorado," he tells his men. They all start to cheer, the realization that they won tonight's battle falling upon them. He points to Diamondback, "You stay close to me. We really do need to talk." Diamondback nods yes. The four men walk out of town into the sunset, Logan joining them. Their own little army follows them. The gold road shimmers in the rising sunlight, but all Cap can think about is being able to see the golden city of El Dorado.

Chapter 7

The rain falls softly upon the mountain trail. Sunlight shows through the gray clouds, but the cloud cover doesn't show any sign of letting the sun through. Luke, Martine, and her werecat pride move slowly on this very wet and cold morning. Despite the weather, birds are singing in every direction, oblivious to the group's existence. It is peaceful, as if Mother Nature didn't know about the pain and turmoil that will inevitably occur.

Luke walks slowly through the mud. The black fur coat Martine gave him is keeping his body dry and warm. His mind isn't interested in the weather or the chill of the wind though. He's concentrating on the werecats. He's seen them transform into large cats. Many of them look like bobcats, mountain lions, jaguars, even really large house cats. Somehow, every part of their bodies in human form also becomes an important or visible part of their cat form.

Martine, for example, when she's in her cat form is a large house cat. She has gray fur, with a white belly. Her long fingernails become formidable claws. Her braided hair transforms into her tail, while the few strands that stick out become whiskers upon her face. Martine, in her cat form walks beside Luke, dodging mud puddles effortlessly. He finds it truly amazing how graceful she moves.

They've been walking for two days now. Martine always keeps at least two of her werecats up ahead, scouting for trouble. Luke hasn't seen anything that would be any cause for trouble, but Martine said that there are many demons and deadly creatures that inhabit the forests that can and will do them harm. The leokampois for example, a fish tailed lion, lives in this area. So she says anyways. It's something Luke cannot believe, but finds himself trying to stay alert for it.

Martine changes into her human form as they enter a clearing in the forest. "We are in the Bergsrå Mountains," she tells him, "We're almost to the Upinis River. We'll follow the river northwest to Lake Eżerinis."

"Sure," Luke responds automatically, "Anyway, can we get something to eat. I haven't had a bite to eat in God only knows how long." His stomach rumbles for added effect.

Martine laughs, "We can stop for lunch here." She turns to two of the werecats behind her, "Larry, Jaime, you two go out and get us some food. We'll camp here for lunch." The two cats bound off into the forest. "Find some wood to make a fire, Luke. I know how you humans don't like to eat meat raw."

Luke's stomach rumbles again in disappointment at the sound of meat. He walks off into the forest, filling his arms with wood. He tries to only pick up dead wood, knowing it will light on fire better, and produce less smoke than pieces that are still green. 'Just a few days ago I was chasing Cap through a forest fire. Now I'm gathering wood to light a fire in a forest!' He laughs out loud at the thought, unknowingly attracting the attention of a leokampoi up the mountain.

With his arms are overloaded with wood, he heads back towards the clearing. The werecats in their human form already had a fire built as he enters the area. He begins to walk to them, when they all transform immediately. He stops as he hears a branch snap behind him. He turns around slowly to see a huge lion. The animal is almost as tall as he is, and at least 500 pounds! Luke backs up slowly. The cat steps out of the brush, its dark mane flowing in the breeze. Luke almost laughs through his fear when its tail shows. The tail looks like a trout's, fin and all. The leokampoi hunches down, never taking its eyes off of Luke. Martine yells something at him, and he turns his head towards her. She tackles him, rolling him out of the way of the pouncing lion.

The werecat pride attacks the beast as one. Clawing and biting they fight the much larger, dangerous animal. The leokampoi fights back, throwing all of them off. It grabs a jaguar looking werecat by the neck, killing it quickly and throwing it behind it towards the trees. The werecats attack again, but more wearily. They focus on staying out of reach, and only attacking when the beast is concentrated on another werecat. Slowly, they begin to back the leokampoi into the forest. It backs up, then turns around and walks to the dead werecat. It picks up the carcass, and runs into the woods.

Luke sits on the ground, stunned by what he has just witnessed. Martine is beside him, "Till you begin to change, you're not going into the forest alone ever again."

He looks at her, forgetting everything that just happened, "What do you mean?"

Martine smiles coldly, "We gave you the potion to drink so you can understand all the languages of Immortalis. You will become one of three things. A werecat, a werewolf, or a vampire. But if you become a werewolf, we *will* have to kill you. They are our greatest threats. They ambush us, we attack them. A cat and dog thing is the easiest way to explain it."

"Couldn't you or Breanna just have bitten me? Isn't that the way it's supposed to be done?" he asks.

"Yes, and no," she explains, "If you are bitten, you will turn into the creature that had bit you, but you will be under the control of the one who bites you. When you change by potion, you keep your free will."

"Is that what Breanna meant?"

"That is exactly what she meant. We've given you great power. Your strength will greatly exceed that of your enemies." she tells him.

Luke smiles at the thought, "Cap won't have a chance."

"Cap?" Martine asks.

"The man I'm here to kill," he answers.

She smiles with understanding. She gets up and helps Luke to his feet. The werecats Larry and Jaime enter the clearing from the south, dragging a deer behind them. They drag it close to the fire, and begin skinning it. They start cutting the meat, and try to throw it on the fire. Luke catches it out of the air and sinks his teeth into it, too hungry to care whether it is cooked or not. All the werecats laugh. Luke smiles embarrassed, showing his bloody teeth. They cut a couple more pieces, and throw them onto the fire. Then all the cats are upon the deer, eating everything but the bones. After they all finish eating, they all settle down to rest. They gossip, or take catnaps. When they all feel rested, the pride gets up and continues on their journey.

The trail gets thinner as they continue walking in single file west. They come to a few cliffs where Luke has to keep his back against the cliff wall to progress forward, while the werecats walk across without a problem. The trees get thicker as they get closer to the river. Luke can hear the rapid flowing water hitting the rocks as it flows.

As they clear the trees, Luke stares in astonishment. The Upinis River flows very fast on the steep slope of the mountain. It's about a mile wide, and he can only imagine how deep. The rocks jutting out of the water are sharp and jagged, eroded from the fast paced waters.

"Come on," Martine says to everyone, leading the way up stream.

They follow the river for miles. Sometimes they are forced to climb steep hills and small cliffs. It is early evening when they finally reach Lake Eżerinis. The lake is located in a large mountain valley. It stretches about three to five miles in width north to south. As for its length? It ends on its east side, where the river begins, and goes on past the horizon to the west. There is no end within sight.

Martine continues to walk west along the southern shore. Luke can't help but notice the northern shore is a tall cliff, covered with pine trees at the top. The southern shore is very sandy, ash and pine trees lining the beach about a hundred yards from the water.

Martine finally stops after they plodded a few hundred yards in the sand. "Here, Luke, is where you will call on the Leviathan. You must walk out until the water is up to your chest, and then call out for it. If it is curious in you, it will show. Tell it your reason for you waking it from its slumber. If it finds you worthy, it will join you, and us." she tells him.

Luke looks across the water, "Are you sure about this?"

"It doesn't matter if I'm sure about it or not. Cronus is." she answers sternly.

"Ok, let's do this," Luke says. He pulls off his boots and takes his shirt off. He wades out into the cold water, looks back unsurely, and continues out into the water. Martine stands on the beach, never taking her eyes off of him. His back is towards her. She can see his body shiver in the cold water. He gets about waste deep when his body goes under. Martine holds her breath for a moment. Luke appears again, swimming forward to a higher part, and then continues to wade forward till the water is almost up to his neck.

Luke places his hands around his mouth and yells across the lake, "Leviathan! My name is Luke. Come to me." He waits for a couple of minutes, then calls again, "Leviathan! Come to me!"

Martine is disappointed standing on the shore. This man must not be worthy. She's about to walk away when she hears a monstrous roar. It stands out of the water suddenly, standing close to twenty feet above the water. The Leviathan is massive! Its mouth has to be six feet long, with long sharp teeth. Its eyes are placed on its head similar to a horse, allowing it to view not only what is ahead, but what's behind also. The blue scales shimmer as the water runs down its long neck. Its back looks like a small blue island in the large lake.

Martine watches in both awe and bewilderment as it brings its head to eye level with Luke. She can see Luke talking to it. However, she can't hear what he is saying. She watches for several minutes, growing bored, but not daring to stop watching. Suddenly it rears up out of the water, showing its long clawed, webbed feet. It dives its head into the water and picks Luke up before its body hit's the water. All the werecats are forced to run to higher ground as a large wave consumes the beach. Martine turns around in time to see Luke riding on its shoulders. Its long flat tail moves from side to side quickly as the two speed east with the river. She turns into her cat form, running to catch up and follow. She hears Luke yell excitedly when she gets closer, "Year!"

Chapter 8

Cap's army moves east along the gold road. They walk, but they walk hurriedly. Everyone in the group knows that they will need shelter, and a place to stand their ground if the vampire force comes after them. Someone is always looking behind, afraid that there will be something chasing after them. Cap is no different.

He is fully aware that he insulted Breanna, and believes she will come after him and his men with a vengeance. He looks behind the group continuously. Every time he does, he can see the men getting more and more nervous. Due to this, he consciously makes every effort not to look back. The few men with him that survived the Battle of Avalon trust his instinct, respect his command, and believe in the decisions he now makes. He doesn't want to disappoint them. To keep his mind off 'what ifs', he takes time to learn about the men who are helping him, and who he is beginning to trust.

Adolf was a firm believer in the fact that werewolves are soldiers of God, a belief found only in the Dark Ages. It was a German philosophy that didn't last very long. His name, he explained, means noble wolf. To him, it's fitting that he became a werewolf. He is now what he believed in, and was persecuted for. Unlike many of the myths that Cap has heard of, Adolf doesn't change only during a full moon, but whenever he chooses to. The change, Adolf emphasized, is painless from human to wolf, but very painful and exhausting from wolf to human. Therefore, he must always be careful when choosing to change his form. During these changes is when he is most vulnerable.

Logan is a cowboy from Montana. He was a drifter, never happy staying in one place for too long. He traveled the grub line from Texas to Montana. He says he met men like Wild Bill Hickock, Wyatt Earp, and many others. He was holed up in Nebraska fighting warriors of the Sioux one night. There, he says, he was attacked by a werecat. He put two slugs into it, and then it transformed into a human and laughed at him. Frightened and unsure of what to do, he lit a stick of dynamite, and escaped during the confusion. From then on he told his story over and over again. All he ever received was laughter and embarrassment at his expense. He was forced to flee into Montana. A religious group of people not far behind him had chased him out of the Dakotas. He was herding strays in the mountains when he was caught in a landslide. When he awoke, he was here in Immortalis.

Diamondback is the one man that intrigues him. A myth in Cap's own time, Diamondback explained most of what Cap already knew, but didn't believe. Diamondback was abducted, and then experimented on. He was chosen because he was "average". Average height, average build, and average age. Just average. The experiments that were done to him made him immune to venom and poison. This explains why the vampire bite didn't affect him. It also gave him the ability to speak with, and understand venomous creatures. Thus explaining the two snakes with him, a diamondback rattlesnake who he calls Stressly, and a black mamba named Aminah. He rescued them both from captivity, and they stay with him by choice. Together, with his love Blaze, they traveled the earth as mercenaries.

He was a hero, and even worshipped by a few groups around the world, which made him a living god. After his death, he found himself here. He was placed in the dungeon of Avalon for foul language, and volunteered to help. Now, he is giving his loyalty to the people of Avalon. He emphasized that he's only giving it because Cap offered him the choice. Something he respects very deeply.

Finally, there's Merlin. His story is both known, and yet a mystery.

He won't explain it though. He chooses to remain silent, leaving his past up to Cap's imagination. He considers himself only as a guide and advisor.

Cap looks ahead into the distance. He can see a village up ahead. This will be the third one they've came to today. They're just small farming towns, but word of the Vampiric Army has already spread to them. Most of the villagers have already fled, but those who have stayed behind offered them food, and a place to rest. He expects this town will be no different. With Cap's insistence, all who had stayed behind travel with them, carrying any weapon they could get a hold of. Due to this, Cap's force of about twenty men is now a small army of almost one hundred. A little less than the amount of men he had in Avalon.

As they get closer, Cap can see a young boy standing at the edge of the town. After a couple minutes the boy notices the small army, and runs quickly into the town. People gather quickly at the road leading into town. Cap slows his pace, everyone following his lead. He doesn't want them to think they are the enemy, so he's giving them time to study his group. An effort to prematurely stop any possible conflict. When he was close enough to distinguish faces, conflict was the last thing on their minds. What he did see is hope.

A tall man, who appears to be the leader of the town walks out to meet them. His bald head and grey beard show both age and experience, but his posture and muscles still shows signs of youth. "Welcome my friends," he says, "We have been waiting for you. Food and drinks are ready for you. As well as a place to rest, if you would like."

Cap answers the man, "Thank you, sir. That is very hospitable of you. We accept your hospitality greatly. These men are well deserved of it."

"Yes, sir," the man says, "Follow me, please." Cap steps aside and allows his group to follow the man, falling in behind them when the last man passes. Adolf and Diamondback stay behind with him. Logan has disappeared, and is nowhere to be seen.

"Sir Casey," Adolf says smiling, "Don't you think we're wasting too much time?"

Cap answers with a scowl, "For the last time, call me Cap. And no, I don't think we are. These men have been up all night fighting, and on the road since dawn. I think a little food and rest isn't too much to allow them. You don't agree?"

"I do," Adolf replies, "but it's almost midafternoon. If we get caught in the night by Breanna, we might as well consider ourselves dead."

"I don't think so," Diamondback says, "She won't come after us tonight. She's smarter than that."

"See," Cap says to Adolf confidently, yet he is unsure what Diamondback is talking about. He looks back at Diamondback, "Explain, please."

Diamondback smiles at him, "Because you scare her. You out maneuvered her during the battle. She now knows you prepare too well. Her attacks are supposed to surprise and cause confusion with fear. You disrupted that. When she attacks again, she will be sure to have a back-up plan. Just in case you out think her again."

Cap frowns, "Just great. Something else I'll have to account for. Why couldn't they just keep it the same? It would be easier."

Adolf laughs, "That it would. That it would." They follow their men into the center of town, where the townspeople had set up tables and chairs for them. The three of them look at the food with envious eyes. The thought of food and rest is very appealing to all of them right now.

Cap waits till Diamondback and Adolf pass to find seats along the tables. He stands there watching all the men proudly. They had fought all night, and walked all day, and still laughing and joking while they ate. They haven't complained, at least not where he could hear it. Still, he finds himself wondering how he is lucky enough to have such brave men fighting beside him.

Adolf walks up to Cap, worry upon his face, "Cap, we mustn't stay long."

"Just give them some time. They've earned it." He responds.

They are interrupted by the tall man who offered them this hospitality. "I must apologize for so little," he says to Cap, "but we are a small village, and have few supplies to spare."

Cap looks at the man warmly, "There is no need to apologize. What you have done for my men is more than enough. I'm not sure we will be able to repay you."

"My son," the man tells him, "My son would like to join you. If your quest brings honor and peace to this land, I would be more than willing to offer my blessing."

Cap looks at the man astonished, "How old is your son?"

"He will be fifteen this year."

Cap thinks for a moment, choosing his words carefully. "I must refuse. It isn't that we don't need your son. We need all the volunteers we can get. I just cannot allow a young man that young to join our forces. If something were to happen , I could never forgive myself. Nor could I ask for yours and your family's forgiveness. The boy deserves to live a full life. Let him get older and wiser before he makes a decision of that magnitude. At least another year or two. I hope you understand."

The man tries to hide a smile, forcing his voice to sound disappointed. "I will tell him," the man says, and walks away.

Cap watches the man walk proudly to his small cottage. He turns around, and begins searching for a seat among his men. He unconsciously picks up the sound of footsteps coming up behind him.

"That was nice of you." A woman's voice says from behind him.

Cap's eyes never leave the search as he speaks, "Maybe, but I don't like the idea of someone that young being so ready to kill. And no parent should feel obligated to send their child off to war."

"A good sentiment," the voice says, "There is a seat open to your left, Sir Casey. I will see you in El Dorado."

Cap's eyes come up quickly from the tables. He turns around, but no one is there. He searches the crowd behind him for anyone who might have spoken to him, but all he sees are men hurrying about. Turning around again, he finds the open seat, and begins eating.

He eats as fast as he can, knowing he'll be interrupted at any moment. He doesn't have to wait long. Diamondback comes up to him as he stuffs a bread roll into his mouth.

"Cap," he says, "we need to get moving."

Cap takes a large drink from the cup in front of him. "Yeah. Get everyone ready. Let's get out of here." he says.

Diamondback leaves, stopping at every table, letting the men know it's time to go. Cap goes to the man who welcomed them to the town. He shows an air of command, but signs of worry too.

"Sir," Cap says to him, "I insist that you all accompany us to El Dorado. It will be safer for all of you there."

"Some of us wish to stay. We need to protect our homes," the man answers.

"I wouldn't suggest that, "Logan says walking up quickly and breathing hard. "It looks like a few werecats already started scouting our trail. They've begun torching everything left behind."

"Oh joyous," Cap says sarcastically. He looks back at the man, "Get everyone ready now. We're all leaving." The man lowers his head, then nods and walks away.

Cap looks at Logan, exhaustion showing on his face. "Zombies, vampires, imps, and now werecats? What else should I be expecting?" he asks.

"Don't ask," Logan says seriously, "You don't want to know the answer."

Cap shakes his head and walks to the other end of town. The townspeople rush around him, grabbing what they can before they leave. He makes his way in front of his men and looks back. The town had more people than he had expected. His force of about a hundred when they arrived now looks like an army of two hundred. He can hardly believe it.

When it looks like everyone is ready, he turns around and starts walking at a brisk pace. Everyone follows. It's an almost cheery walk. The townspeople laugh and joke, at times they sing songs while they walk. After a few miles, they quiet down, aware of their escorts' nervous looks behind them. What was once cheery, has now become a very dismal walk.

Cap concentrates on not looking back. After a couple more miles, he hears a loud 'crack'. He stops immediately, everyone stopping with him. Adolf is about to speak, but Cap puts a hand up to stop him. They wait in silence for a moment. Just as Cap is about to begin walking, he hears it again. It came from the North!

"Logan, Adolf, Merlin. Come with me." Cap orders, "Diamondback, quicken the pace and get everyone out of here." He takes off running north, not waiting for an answer.

He tops a hill and stops, mouth wide open and panting. What he sees he can't explain. He just points as the rest catch up to him. On the large plain in front of him, two large creatures are battling each other. Both look like very tall humans, but one looks white as snow and ice, the other the multiple colors of fire. The fire creature throws a fire ball, landing it against the ice creature's shoulder. A deafening 'crack' is heard from the impact.

"Ifrit, the fire genie," Merlin explains. The ice creature shoots a stream of ice at the Ifrit, causing steam and rain all around. "Agoolik, the ice spirit," the magician informs him.

They watch as the Agoolik continues its stream of ice. The ice surrounds the Ifrit, dulling its fire and weakening the genie. The Ifrit falls down, looking more and more human as the fire slowly goes out. The Agoolik shows no remorse, intentions of ending their battle then and there. Cap runs to help the Ifrit, unable to watch the helpless genie's life be extinguished. He thrusts Adflictus in front of the ice stream, reflecting it back at the Agoolik.

The Agoolik dodges the stream, stopping its own attack on the Ifrit. "That was unwise," it tells Cap.

"It is dishonorable to finish off a helpless enemy," Cap replies.

The Agoolik laughs, "Foolish but noble, mortal."

"Maybe," is all Cap says, preparing to fight as the spirit walks towards him.

It stands in front of him, looking down upon him, "You would fight me to save him?" the Agoolik asks.

"If I have to," answers Cap.

Agoolik lifts its head and laughs very loudly. "I believe you," it says, "I'll let the fire genie live, for now. We will meet again. Hopefully on less hostile terms." It lifts its hands and a North wind blows across the plain. The wind forces Cap to cover his eyes. When the wind subsides, he uncovers them. The ice spirit is gone. Cap turns to the Ifrit. It is covered in ice from its feet to its neck. Its body looks completely human, except its head which remains on fire.

"Thank you," it says, "I owe you my life. I shall be your servant until a time comes that I can return the favor." It closes its eyes tightly and its fire burns fiercely, melting the ice around its body. The Ifrit's body slowly turns back to fire as each piece of ice melts away from it. It stands up when all the ice is gone.

Cap waits. When the creature looks back at him, he finally speaks. "You don't owe me your life," Cap says, "I won't be the master of a slave. I won't accept it."

The Ifrit nods in understanding. He holds out his hand, holding something inside of it. It waits for Cap to hold out his hand to receive it. "Then I offer a gift," it tells Cap, dropping a small pebble in his hands. "Keep this with you always. A token of my appreciation." The Ifrit spins suddenly, disappearing into the air. Cap looks at the pebble in his hand. It's small, black, and very smooth. He places it in his pocket as his companions walk up to him.

Logan smiles at him, "You have guts, kid. Lots of guts." Cap just shrugs his shoulders.

Adolf points at the setting sun, "We have to run. If we run, we might make it before they close the gates." Adolf takes off running, the rest trying to keep up. "El Dorado is only a mile away. We can make it." He calls out behind him. They run hard and fast. They can see El Dorado shine in the fading light as they top a hill, the sun's rays making the golden city seem to glow. They run straight to the gate, only to find it closed.

"Let us in," Adolf calls out.

"No entrance after the sun is down," a guard from behind the gate informs. Cap can't believe it. He looks behind him to the west. The sun is just below the horizon.

"Let them in," a deep voice behind the wall orders. The gates open, and they are greeted by a very muscular, dark skinned man. "So," the man says, "it is possible for a human to survive The Vampiric Army. Your story has already made it across the land. Sir Casey, I am Sir Palomedes the

Saracen. Welcome to El Dorado."

 Cap smiles, and then hit's the ground. He is passed out cold with exhaustion.

Chapter 9

Black. That is all Cap can see through his eye lids. It is all he wants to see. His muscles are sore, and he can feel weakness from exhaustion throughout his entire body. He opens his eyes, unable to keep them closed any longer. He's in an extremely dim lit room. He sits up in bed, studying the room. The furniture seems to be from seventeenth century Spain. The dresser, mirror, table, and chair all have bold mixtures of wood, gold, and iron. The dresser sits directly across from the bed, a mirror above it. Below the window stands a table, with a small lamp on top of it. Beside it to the right sits a very luxurious chair. He can't help but wonder at his luck of waking into such a wealthy room.

The door opens slowly, and a young woman with dark hair walks into the room. Her emerald gown is form fitting upon her upper body, with sleeves that go down to her wrists. She wears an undershirt that laces out at her wrists. The skirt is bowed out from her waste, stopping just short of the floor. She walks very softly to the window, and lights the lamp on the table beneath it. Not noticing that Cap is watching her, she places clothes upon the chair. Quietly, she walks over to the dresser. She pours water into a basin, then folds a couple towels and places them next to it.

Cap sits there, unsure of what to do or say. They lady turns away from the dresser and looks at him. They stare at each other for a moment before she speaks. "I have been asked to wake you. When you have cleaned up and dressed, you are asked to join the town elders for supper. I will wait outside till you are ready." She tells him.

She turns and begins to leave the room when he stops her. "Wait!" he calls out to her.

"Yes, my lord?"

"How long have I been asleep?"

She smiles amusingly before she speaks, "For a full night and all day, my lord." She walks out the door, closing it behind her.

Cap sits there for a moment, and then throws the blankets off of him. He notices that he's only in his boxers. 'Not again,' he thinks. He gets out of bed very slowly, noticing sore muscles that he didn't know he had. He waddles with his sore muscles over to the dresser and washes his face and upper body. He dries himself off and goes to the chair and gets dressed.

He looks out the window as he dresses. He can see the sun slowly lowering in the sky, but the people along the street keep working and moving along. They walk as if they don't have a care in the world. It's almost conceivable that they don't believe that any trouble could interfere with their lives. He looks upon the serene scene with both hope and sorrow. He knows that their lives will be changed forever very soon.

A gold chain on the table suddenly catches his eye. Embraced in gold upon the chain is the black pebble that the Ifrit had given him. He puts it around his neck, hiding it beneath his shirt. Putting the boots on that were provided for him, he finishes dressing and goes to the mirror above the dresser. He looks at himself and smiles. The shirt is black, with flamboyant colors of red, white, blue, and green in intricate patterns all around it. His pants are also black, with no colors. His boots are black also, but freshly polished. He smiles at himself in the mirror. He contrasts with the gold walls, but he cannot help but think he looks good.

He walks out of the room, stopping outside the doorway. "I think we are ready to go," he tells the lady.

She nods her head, and leads the way out of the small house. Cap follows closely, a little to her right just in case she stops abruptly. After a little while his eyes wander, staring in awe as he looks at the golden city. It is massive in size. Far larger than he could have ever expected it to be. Just to make things even grander, every inch of it is made with gold! Streets, buildings, walls, and even statues! It all shines with gold!

He doesn't notice the woman is trying to drag him along. He's lost in amazement and awe. That is until she almost throws him to the ground. He looks at her, very embarrassed. "I'm very sorry, ma'am," he says, "I guess I got lost in the moment. It's just that I've never seen anything like this before!"

She tries to hide her amusement as they continue walking. "No need to apologize, my lord," she tells him.

He frowns at that. "Please, call me Cap. Being called 'lord' is just too formal for my blood." She laughs out loud, unable to hold it in. He looks at her, confused for a second. He smiles, understanding the humor. "May I ask what your name is?"

"Isabella," she tells him, composing herself.

"Well, Isabella, it's a pleasure to meet you," he says.

"The pleasure is mine, Sir Casey."

"Please, it's just Cap."

"Forgive me, my lord. You have been knighted, you are the commander of Avalon, and have survived the Vampiric Army. It would be disrespectful of me not to acknowledge that. You've earned the titles. The least I can do is show respect for all of that." she tells him.

Cap frowns at the thought. 'I'll never be able to live this one down,' he thinks. He knows that he might as well get used to it. "Alright," he says discouragingly, "I'll allow it."

She laughs again, leading him up the steps of a large building. He follows her through a hallway to a set of large gold doors. She opens the doors, allowing Cap to enter a large room. An empty room, except for the two men waiting for him inside. He recognizes Sir Palomedes immediately, his dark skin standing out in the bright gold room. The other man he doesn't recognize. He has a brown beard, and what Cap can only describe as conquistador armor. The doors close behind him, and hears Isabella move aside, standing quietly along the wall.

Sir Palomedes sees him and waves him over. "Sir Casey! It's good to see you. We've been hoping you weren't too overwhelmed on your journey," he says, "I'd like you to meet Captain Juan Gonzalez, commander of El Dorado."

"It's an honor sir," Cap says, shaking the man's hand.

"Likewise," the captain responds.

Cap looks around the room as he speaks to him them, "I may be asking too much, but is it possible for you two to just call me Cap?"

Sir Palomedes smiles at him as he answers, "I cannot. It is not your title, or your name."

"I thought as much. It was worth a try," Cap says, "I thought we were going to have dinner? The room is empty."

In answer, the doors open and servants bring in a table and chairs. They follow that quickly with dishes of food. The three men stand aside as they watch the servants prepare everything. Dishes of cereal, potatoes, and maize are placed around the table. A large roast is placed in the center of the table, still steaming. The servants also pour a red wine into each of the cups. The servants work quickly and diligently, putting everything in its proper place with meticulous order and precision. After everything is set, the servants hurry to leave the room.

Shortly after, three older looking gentlemen come into the room. They sit down, motioning for the three to sit also. The three elders sit together, as do the three commanders. Only one seat remains empty between Captain Gonzalez and one of the elders. It is directly across from Cap, who can't help but wonder who the seat is for.

"Captain Gonzalez, Sir Palomedes, Sir Casey," the elder in the middle greets them, interrupting Cap's thoughts, "We are pleased that you have been able to join us. I'm sure you all have more pressing matters to deal with. But, we believe that what has happened in Avalon needs explanation. Explanation for all of us, so that we all may know what is ahead for all of us."

Cap's face shows many emotions as his thoughts go back. "Where would you like me to begin, sir?" he asks.

A woman's voice carries across the room from behind Cap, "From the very beginning, Sir Casey."

Cap stands up and turns around, immediately recognizing the voice from the village. He is shocked in awe at who he sees. To him, she's the most beautiful woman he's ever seen. She's about medium height, around five feet and five inches he guesses, and a very slim figure. Her eyes are a gorgeous blue, and curly blonde hair hangs down below her shoulders. Her hair is held back by a band of blue flowers. Her facial features seem perfect. From her high cheek bones to her very light, soft skin. She wears a baby blue toga, with shades of purple throughout the cloth. She shines like a diamond, making the gold room look very plain. She moves more gracefully than Cap has ever seen anyone move as she walks to the empty seat. He can't help but stare. Everything about her seems perfect.

"Gentlemen, please sit," she tells them as she sits down herself. Cap sits suddenly aware that he wasn't the only one standing.

The elder next to him speaks, "Athena, I'm happy to see that you are able to join us."

"Thank you for waiting. My apologies for being late," she says, "Please, Sir Casey, tell us about the battle from the beginning."

"Yes. Um…" Cap looks around the table, turning red with embarrassment, "I'm sorry. I don't know the proper way to address a goddess."

She smiles at him, "Athena is just fine, for now."

"Yes, Athena," he says unsure of himself, "but I must ask about my men. I haven't yet been given the opportunity to check on them yet."

"I have made sure that they were given food, drink, and a place to rest," Sir Palomedes tells him.

"Your men are well cared for," Captain Gonzalez adds, "Please, tell us of the battle."

Cap takes a deep breath, and then tells the story as best as he could remember. From noticing that the army wasn't going to make a long siege, to the king knighting him and giving him command. He explained why he gave the orders of resting the men, and lighting every light within the city. He told of Adolf leaving, and meeting Breanna and Salma. Then he explained the battle with as much detail as possible, taking time to explain how each soldier's placement was tactical. He finished the story with him holding Breanna to the ground, and giving up Avalon.

They give him a moment to collect his thoughts. Then the elder in the middle speaks to him. "Tell me. Why didn't you stay and defend Avalon?"

"It would have been murder for my men, sir," Cap responds, "We might have been able to fight it out during the day, but they would have been slaughtered when night fell. They gave up everything to allow their family and friends time to escape. It is the least I could do to allow them to see their loved ones again."

"And about Breanna and Salma?" Athena asks, "Why did you allow them to live?"

"Besides the fact that it was part of the deal, it was something I noticed about her," Cap says, "I don't know if it was something I saw, or felt, but something within her seems honorable and virtuous. She also cares about her army. I thought she would be less dangerous than a commander willing to sacrifice his or her entire army for just one objective."

"Let's hope you are right," the elder on the left says, "If you're not, we will all have hell to pay."

"Gentlemen," Athena speaks up, "We should be congratulating this man. We shouldn't be criticizing him for his success. He gained his objective, and then some." The elders didn't say anything, but frowned, obviously upset about Cap's decisions.

"Thank you," Cap says to Athena, "But, it wasn't all success. I wasn't supposed to survive the fight."

She just smiles, knowing something that he doesn't. "That isn't a decision for you to make, but fate's. Your destiny is probably farther down the road." she tells him.

"Maybe," is all Cap says.

Athena leans against the table. "I would like to make a recommendation to the elders, and yourselves," she tells all of them. The elders look up, an almost disgust look in their eyes. She continues without noticing, "I think Sir Palomedes and his knights should return to King Arthur. He needs to hear of all this right away. Captain Gonzalez should protect El Dorado. As much as possible anyways. I would like it if Sir Casey and his army could escort me to Shambhala. It would be greatly appreciated. If it would please the elders to do so, of course."

The three older men look at each other, but say nothing. Finally, the elder in the middle speaks, "We must discuss it. We need some time to make a decision."

Athena smiles proudly at them. "Of course. We will wait outside while you discuss it." She stands up, all the men standing up with her, and walks out of the room. The three commanders and Isabella follow behind her.

Isabella closes the doors, and they wait. Everyone remains quiet at first. Yet, after a few moments, Athena begins to laugh quietly. Everyone looks at her, confused as to what she is laughing at. Cap found himself wanting to ask, but with everyone else remaining silent, he's not sure if he should. Athena doesn't stop laughing, and Cap's curiosity grows bolder. He cannot stop himself.

"Athena? I'm sorry, but could you tell me what you're laughing about?" Cap asks. Sir Palomedes and Captain Gonzalez look at him incredulously. They seem surprised that he would question the goddess, yet curious themselves.

"You don't see it?" She asks him. Cap shakes his head no. "It's El Dorado! The city of gold! These elders have never been warriors, or heroes of any kind. More like old bankers. Greedy old men who believe that holding riches also holds power. They are in charge of the golden city, so any suggestion, even from a god or goddess is an insult to them. Of course, they can't say no either. They are still human. They cannot depose a god. So they are stuck between their own egos and humility. I find it very funny."

Cap smiles, but he doesn't quite see the humor in it. He decides to stand in silence, and wait until the elders make a decision. He looks at the two commanders with him. Each is a very capable leader and warrior also. But what about him?

This causes him to wonder why Athena asked for him as an escort. It would have made more sense to ask for either one of them. He looks at the goddess. 'On the other hand, it would be a great honor,' he thinks to himself.

After a few minutes of silence, the doors open. They all walk back inside, Cap appearing more anxious than his companions for the elders answer. Only after they had seated themselves, would any one of the elders look at them.

The elder in the middle is the first to speak. "We have made our decision," he says to Athena, "We have decided that it would be better if Sir Palomedes and his knights escort you. We will keep Sir Casey and his army here, under Captain Gonzalez's command. El Dorado must be protected at all cost. We cannot let it fall into the hands of the Vampiric Army." The three men sit up very proudly as the elder finishes speaking.

Athena's face becomes very stern. "No," she says with authority, "El Dorado is not the most important city in Immortalis. It is not the richest. It does not need to be protected." Her voice gets louder and angrier as she goes on. "Sir Casey WILL escort me to Shambhala. Sir Palomedes MUST take this news to the king. Captain Gonzalez NOW knows how to defend the city from the Vampiric Army. He and his forces will protect the people of El Dorado, NOT El Dorado itself!" Her face begins to get red with anger as the three men whisper amongst each other.

"That is not what we decided," the elder on the right says, "As the elders here, we must see to the needs of the city."

Athena smiles coldly at the old men. "And you consider Sir Palomedes and Sir Casey citizens of El Dorado?" she asks.

"Of course not!" the elder on the left says immediately, "They could never be citizens of our grand city."

"Then, as neither Sir Palomedes nor Sir Casey are citizens of El Dorado, they do not have to abide by your decision," she tells them. The three men's smug smiles turn to deep frowns as they realize the trap they had just entered. "Sir Casey," says Athena directing her gaze to him, "Would the forces of Avalon be willing to escort me to Shambhala?"

"It would be an honor," Cap replies to her, "We would be pleased to escort you."

Athena turns to Sir Palomedes. "And you? Do you not think that King Arthur should be informed about these recent events?"

"Yes, my lady," Sir Palomedes says, "I do believe that the king should be informed."

"Then it is settled," Athena says before the elders can make any argument. She turns her head to Isabella in the back of the room, and nods her head to her. She turns back to the table as Isabella leaves the room. "Now, is there any questions?" she asks, directing her gaze towards the elders.

"No," they answer disappointed in unison. They all look very disappointed. It is the one in the middle who continues speaking, "If you would please excuse us. We have important matters to tend to. Enjoy the meal. It is Immortalis' best." The three men stand and leave the room very quickly.

Athena smiles at her victory. "Eat, gentlemen. You will all need the strength," she tells them.

They all begin eating. Cap realizes why the elders said it was the best food in Immortalis. He cannot remember ever eating anything that has tasted this good. He eats quickly, but consciously eats slow enough to taste every bite. He's concentrating so hard on the food, that he doesn't notice Isabella walking back into the room. It is a few more moments before he feels the eyes of everyone in the room upon him. He looks up to see that everyone is looking at him.

"Sir Casey," Athena says, "As a token of appreciation for defending the people of Avalon, the gods would like to offer you a gift." Isabella walks up to him holding a small shield. It is about a foot and a half tall, and eight inches in width at the top. Its top is straight, and the sides curve down to a point at the bottom. On the shield are an eagle and a lion side by side. Both are colored a shining orange, the same as Adflictus. The two animals are separated by a gold diagonal line. The line separates the yellow upper shield from the deep red on the lower. On the back of the shield are two adjustable leather straps, for Cap to place his arm through.

Cap is stunned. "I-I don't know what to say," he stammers.

"Say yes," Athena replies.

"Yes. Thank you very much," he says.

"Here," says Sir Palomedes, "let me help you with it." Cap nods his head in silent approval. Sir Palomedes holds the shield up as Cap places his left arm through the straps, adjusting them to fit tightly upon his arm. Sir Palomedes steps back to look at Cap and his shield. It sits about two inches above his arm, and hangs down. It is surprisingly light. Where it sits on his arm, he's able to move his wrist. This should allow him to use his weapon with both hands without interference from the shield.

"That's more like it," Athena says, "A knight should have a shield worthy of his character. It was made by Hephaestus himself. It cannot be penetrated or bent. Now you just need the right suit of armor to go with it. Go see the blacksmith, then prepare your men. We leave at first light in the morning."

"Yes, ma'am," Cap says, and watches her leave the room, Isabella directly behind her. He looks at the shield again. It feels like it has already become an extension of his arm. He looks at his companions and can only imagine what will happen next.

Chapter 10

Breanna watches from the castle in Avalon as the imps bring the dead back to life in Avalon. The battle two days before had depleted her army, both zombies and vampires. Since then, the imps have been working around the clock to replenish the forces. They preferred to wait, raising the dead too soon is a very dangerous task, but they must to get numbers back to where they need to be.

She too has been working to replenish her vampires' numbers. She has been scouring the country side and villages for any of the free willed humans. Many of whom chose to become one of her vampires, as opposed to becoming one of the zombies. The population is far too low though. This Cap had gone through the villages during his retreat from Avalon. Unfortunately, he took almost everyone with him. It is because of this that talk of attacking El Dorado prematurely is occurring. The city will have plenty of live humans, and dead, after they attack it. Their spy within the city has informed the werecats scouting the town that the citizens have chosen to defend the city. What was also mentioned was that Cap and his men, along with the Knights of the Round Table, will be leaving in the morning. She finds this relieving, as Cap has out maneuvered her once already.

How he had guessed her moves during the battle she has no idea. She had assumed that the soldiers of Avalon would do what they had always done, but Cap taking command had made different decisions. That difference alone was costly and devastating. The "intimidate and attack" tactics she had always used in previous victories doesn't even seem to faze the mortal. Her being the most powerful vampire in Immortalis alone should have had him shivering with fear. It didn't.

She shakes her head, trying to discard the negative thoughts. She needs to be thinking about the upcoming plans on El Dorado. The knights are supposed to leave, as well as Cap, but she can't be sure until it actually happens. So what would be the most advantageous? Her normal tactics? The man who could stay one step ahead will be gone. A siege maybe? Choking them out of their supplies till they are forced to negotiate? That could take days, possibly months.

On the other hand, it could minimize casualties on both sides, mainly her side. She could also use their greed against them. The town isn't anything important. It is just a stepping stone to the final destination. If she offered the town to be allowed to rule itself, they might agree, with certain stipulations of course. Swearing fealty to Cronus is a definite, as well as the governor she appoints.

But what stipulations could she make? Should she force some of them to become vampires, or ask for volunteers? If by force or willingness, how many would be sufficient? Twenty-five percent? Fifty? The dead won't have a choice. They will become zombies so there's no need to think about that. That might have to wait till the time comes. Yet, it is something that needs to be kept in the back of her mind.

She smiles as the plan develops in her head. The more she thinks about it, the more she likes it. They could bring Luke along. Let him get a feel of commanding. With Cap out of the picture, he shouldn't do anything stupid out of rage. He will need the experience for larger targets. That should do very well.

She continues to think about upcoming plans, but her memory takes over. Cap was hers! She would have had him if it weren't for Diamondback! Diamondback, him she cannot understand. That isn't the first encounter with him, but the third. He is the only human that can resist her venom. He is the only mortal she cannot control. That upsets and her greatly. He is a worthy adversary. That also makes him very dangerous to her plans. As long as he's fighting with Cap, there isn't any way she can get close to Cap. Diamondback will interfere every time. This fact leaves her with only two options. She must kill him, or convince him to join her.

What will it be that would bring him over? Money can't be used. El Dorado is the only place where money means anything. Power might work, but he seems content with what he is doing. Still, power is always an influence. If she has to, she could offer half of her army to him. Sharing though, has never been one of her strong points. Yet, if he rejects that, what else could she use? A thought of taking a captive that is very close to him enters her mind. She frowns at the thought. 'That will have to be a last resort,' she thinks.

She looks out the window. The Leviathan is stretched out in the lake. Moonlight shines off of its shiny blue scales. That Cronus has something planned for the beast is evident, but what that secret could be he keeps to himself. She would still like to know its purpose, but she also knows that she'll find out in time.

Time. In this land it is immeasurable. And yet, their plans have already been forced to be readjusted to use more of it. Cap's ability to out think her during the battle caused that. She was too sure of herself. That had to be the fault. It was arrogance in her army's ability and her own ability to command that did it. She won't make that mistake again. Hopefully he doesn't realize that. It could be very devastating for both sides. Cronus wanted a fast victory. The way this might go, it could last years.

She should fly to El Dorado and speak to the spy herself. Information second hand isn't reliable. That should tell her everything. The spy has met Cap in peaceful terms. Her small amount of knowledge about that could be most useful. Yes, that is what she will do. She looks at the moon. It is plenty high enough now.

She leaps out the window and flies eastward. She takes her time, surveying the ground below. She sees burnt fields and smoldering villages. She feels sorrow at the sight. How could Cronus allow such destruction in the land he created? Has his hatred really blinded him from everything else? She finds herself hoping he hasn't. The titan is like a father to her, but lately she finds herself questioning his decisions more often than not. Something just doesn't feel right. She doesn't know what it could be though. It is just that Cronus has been acting odd. She could be mistaken though. She has been shaken up since the battle. She hasn't been herself either.

She stops over a village still glowing red with embers. She lands in the center of town, among overturned tables and chairs. The scent of burned food still remains in the air. She looks through the smoke to the burned buildings. She knows the town was empty when the werecats burned it down, but she can't help but feel sorrowful about it. These were people's homes! Cronus' forces are destroying not only the land its self, but also innocent people's lives and lively hoods. She grabs a table and throws it across town in frustration. 'This isn't the way it is supposed to be!' she thinks to herself. As her breath calms down with her emotions, she could feel the presence of someone behind her.

"To sneak up on a vampire is almost certain death," Breanna says to the person.

"I'm just watching," a young woman's voice replies.

"I thought I would have to find you in town, Isabella," Breanna says to her, "What are you doing here?"

"I wanted to see the damage myself. After all," Isabella responds, "it was promised to me."

Breanna turns around to face her, "That is only if your information is good and useful."

"It is. The Knights of the Round Table leave in the morning. Sir Casey and his men are to escort Athena to Shambhala in the morning also."

"Sir Casey?"

"He prefers to be called Cap, but everyone refuses to. That is, everyone except those closest to him."

"I see. And what is this Sir Casey like?"

"He is polite and caring. Intelligent, and yet, somewhat ignorant. He doesn't know the ways of Immortalis yet. I'm not sure he wants to."

"He knows," Breanna says surely, "He's learning too quickly not to. Do you know how many men will be defending the town?"

"With the villagers Sir Casey brought with him, there will be approximately a thousand defenders."

Breanna thinks about the number for a moment. "Perfect. Half of that will be more than enough to replenish my army."

"And me?"

"Once El Dorado is captured, you will be made governor of the city and its surrounding lands. With your continued service, of course. Once we win this war, you will be made queen with El Dorado and all of the surrounding lands."

"Thank you, Madam."

"Anything else?"

"No, Madam, that is all."

"Very well then. Meet me here tomorrow evening. I will want an update, and you won't want to be in town when the zombies arrive."

"Yes, Madam." Isabella watches Breanna disappear into the night sky. 'After tomorrow,' she thinks, 'I'll be the most powerful human in Immortalis!'

Cap heard the woman behind the door giggle softly before she knocked. His body is still wary, and he didn't sleep much during the night. He doesn't say anything, just lays there hoping for a few more moments of peace. The woman behind the door knocks again, dashing that hope.

He hears the door creep open, and Isabella cautiously sticks her head into the room. "Sir Casey?" she asks timidly, "Sir Casey, you had asked for someone to wake you."

"Yeah," he says, "I'm up. Thank you, Isabella." He can barely see her face in the dim light, but he can't help but note to himself how attractive she looks in it. "Isabella?"

"Yes, my lord," she answers.

"Please, if you would, please just call me Cap," he tells her, "I'm no better than any other person. Not a king or yourself. Would you please do that?"

"I can do that, Cap," she replies.

"Good," he says, "Thank you again."

"You're welcome," she says, and shuts the door.

He gets out of bed, and begins dressing in the moonlight. The reflection of light in the gold room is more than enough. He sees no need to light the lamp. He looks at his new clothing in the dim light. The colors seem darker, but they are still visible.

His pants are a dark red, with small metal plates inserted to protect his shins and thighs. The metal was formed to his legs, so he barely could tell it was there. That is except for the added weight. His shirt is leather and multi colored. It begins at the bottom in deep red and gradually lightens up to an orange from his upper chest to neck. There is a small hole where the black pebble that he wears around his neck fits perfectly in place.

It is sleeveless, except for the small metal shields over the shoulders. The right shoulder has a fire background, with an eagle in the center. The left also has a fire background, but a lion in the center. He puts his black boots on, then straps his shield to his left arm and stands in front of the mirror.

He laughs at himself in the mirror. He looks like he is engulfed in flame! The colors just seem to promote themselves out that way. He isn't sure if that was the blacksmith's and tailor's intention, but it seems to be the way it works out. He takes one last look at himself, smiling with humor, grabs Adflictus, and leaves the room.

Isabella is waiting for him as he steps out. Her eyes get large as she looks him up and down. "Oh my," she says.

"What?" Cap asks, looking at his clothing, "Did I miss something?"

"Oh, no," she answers, "It looks very well on you."

"Well, thank you," he tells her, "Shall we?" He holds out his arm for her. She takes it and begins to lead him through town. Everything feels so peaceful as the town sleeps, excluding those getting ready to depart this morning. He can see his men waiting for him up ahead. Diamondback, Adolf, and Logan are in front of the twenty men group. They stand still, waiting for him to get closer.

"Interesting choice of gear," Logan says to Cap. He turns his attention Isabella, "Could you give us some privacy ma'am. I would appreciate it." Isabella nods her head and walks to the right, over to Athena's chariot. The goddess hasn't arrived as of yet.

Logan waits until she's out of hearing distance before he speaks. "We wanted to speak to you alone about this," he says, "We know you are still new to the land, but we think you've got the hang of things. We've discussed it, and we would like to stay and help out here. I hope you don't mind."

"No," Cap says, "I don't mind. None of you are in any kind of service to me. It's your decision, not mine. Good luck to all of you. Just," he pauses for a brief moment, "just be careful. You have all become friends. I would like to see you all down the road again."

"You be careful as well," Adolf says to Cap, "There's a rumor going around about a spy. No one knows who, but I would bet there is one."

"I would put money on it," Logan says.

"Also," says Diamondback, "Keep your mind on your mission. Not everyone gets the opportunity to escort a deity. Don't let your mind stray. Don't worry about us. We'll be just fine."

"As you wish," Cap says smiling. He shakes each of their hands in turn, then watches them walk away.

He turns around looks over at his men. They were saddling up horses that someone had provided for them. He wasn't aware of this. He thought that they'd be walking the entire way. He smiles at it though. His makeshift infantry is now a cavalry. The irony of the promotion amuses him.

Athena walks up behind Cap as he watches his men prepare. She doesn't say anything, but watches him closely. His clothing makes him stand out from the pale orange uniforms of his men. It identifies him as both commander and individual, yet no one would be able to tell from the way he talks. He's caring of his men, yet stern and deadly to his enemies when he needs to be. The only true thing that is missing is adversity. He's done well so far, but things will get worse before long. She can't help but wonder how he'll face it.

Cap's head straightens up. Isabella has noticed Athena and has begun walking over. Cap turns around to face Athena. He bows to her, imitating others he has seen, and then says, "My lady. How may I be of service to you?"

"Nothing right now. Thank you, Sir Casey," she answers.

"Alright," he says, "may I ask where all these horses come from?"

Isabella answers as she reaches them, "They are gifts from the elders of El Dorado, Cap."

"You will address him with the proper respect, Isabella," Athena says sternly.

Isabella hangs her head, "Yes, my lady."

"It's alright," Cap says quickly, "I've asked her to. I'm more comfortable with it."

"Very well," says the goddess, a sound of disgust in her voice.

Cap looks Athena in the eyes, "I would appreciate it if you would call me that also. You're a goddess. You outrank me in every way. There is no reason why you should be forced to call me by any title."

"It is respectful to call a commander by his, or her, proper title," Athena tells him, "I will call you that. It is the respect you have earned."

Cap lifts his hands in front of him, "Ok, ok. I'm not trying to argue. I'm just not used to all of these formalities."

"It'll come to you. As well as knowledge and wisdom," Athena tells him. She looks to the eastern sky. The first rays of light are beginning to show. "We should be about ready to depart."

"Of course, my lady," Cap says to her, "Please, give me a moment to find a horse." He turns around and begins searching for a lone horse, but they all seem to be taken. He counts them to himself. There is just enough for his men. 'They deserve it,' he thinks, 'but how am I supposed to keep up?'

Athena laughs very softly to herself. "You won't find one," she says smiling. She whistles loudly, then points to the sky.

Cap looks to where she's pointing. His eyes get big as he sees the pterippus gliding down into the town. It lands softly, its wings pushing out air for a moment. On its back, behind the wings sits a saddle. Cap walks up to it, petting it softly. "You remember me, don't you?" It whinnies softly in response to him.

"Pegasus," Isabella says softly to herself, surprised and confused.

"Yes," Athena says, "Pegasus has volunteered his service to help you, Sir Casey. I find it very fitting. Both of you stand out from a crowd, and have the ability to blend in as well. Any commander would be honored to have him as their steed."

"I am," Cap says, "I am deeply honored."

"You will find a special holster on the right side for your weapon," Athena tells him. "Now we should be ready to leave. Yes?"

Cap is about to agree, when he sees the Knights of the Round Table coming up the street. He could see Merlin with them. "Give me just one minute," he tells Athena, and walks away without waiting for an answer.

He meets Merlin in the street, "You going with the knights?" he asks him.

"Yes," Merlin replies, "My place is beside King Arthur."

"I understand. Thank you for everything. The best of luck to you."

"And you also," Merlin says, and then rejoins the knights.

Cap turns around, and walks back to Athena and Isabella. "Ok, I'm ready now." He walks up to Pegasus, petting the winged horse before climbing in the saddle and placing his weapon in its holster. "Mount up," he tells the men. Isabella helps Athena into her carriage, and then nods to the driver. Cap takes the lead as the group moves to the back gate of El Dorado. The guards open the gate before a command can be spoken. As Cap rides out of the city, he turns in the saddle and waves to Isabella. She waves back, smiling at him.

He turns back around and relaxes in the saddle, letting Pegasus walk on its own. The sun is beginning to rise over the horizon, and he marvels at its beauty. 'In a place so beautiful and grand, how can all of this violence occur?' he thinks to himself. As he puzzles for an answer, Athena's carriage pulls up beside him. He doesn't notice, lost in thought.

"Sir Casey?" Athena says to him.

Her voice startles him, but his body doesn't move. "Yes, my lady?"

"It is a long ride to our first resting spot. Would you mind speaking with me for a while?" she asks.

"Not at all," he replies.

"Do you miss your home?"

"I do," he says, thinking back, "but, I really haven't had much time to dwell on it."

"Tell me about it."

"There's not much to tell. I grew up in a fairly large town. The population was about fifty thousand. It was beside three rivers, and trees grew abundant. During the summer, the trees leafed out wondrously, almost blocking the sky from view. In the fall, the leaves turned so many colors it felt that only God could create such beauty. When the snow fell in the winter, everything shimmered and shined. It is like the land itself is covered in shimmering diamonds. And when the flowers and trees bloomed in spring, the sweet scents that flowed just seemed to fill the body."

"It sounds like you miss it more than you thought."

Cap smiles, "I guess I do."

"What do you miss the most about your home?"

"The music. I really miss the music the most. There were so many different kinds, and so many different melodies and harmonies. It always soothed me when I was feeling down."

"And what about your family?"

Cap's smile turned to a frown, "Well, my mother died when I was really young. I don't remember much about her, except that she was very pretty. So it was just my dad, my brother, and me.

"Dad did the best he could to provide for a family on his own. He really was a hero in his own right. More so to me now than then. I don't know how he did it, but he'd always take us to the mountains every summer. He was killed in a hijacking a couple of years ago.

"As for my brother, we are alike only in appearance. I was studying to be a historian, he went into the military. Obviously, we have very different interests. We stayed very close after our father passed. He would stay with me when he came home on leave, and in return he would take me on trips around the world. It wasn't till we had our falling out with each other that anything seemed to go terribly wrong."

"I am sorry," Athena says sadly.

"It's ok," he says to her, forcing a smile to his face, "There's no way you could have known."

"Still…"

"Don't worry about it," he tells her, "What about you? Do you miss Athens and Greece?"

"Yes and no," she says, catching his quick change of subjects away from his past, "In that world I was worshipped, but I could only speak to my people through oracles and high priests. Occasionally, I would be able to assist a great hero. Here, I may not be worshipped as much, but I am able to associate with the people more. I can speak to people with my own words, instead of through another. Here, I am more involved."

"I see," he says, "Quick question. How long does it take to get to Shambhala?"

"Days," she answers.

Cap just nods his head. He stops Pegasus as they top a hill, and looks back. Thunderclouds are building in the western sky. Concern blankets his face. Worries build about his friends. 'I hope they make it,' he thinks, 'They have to.'

The trip to Shambhala has taken four days, and only one of them was on the plains. Two of them were crossing mountain valleys and going around mountains that were too high and rugged for the gold road, or the Hamingja Road, as Athena calls it.

The road was created by the spirit Hamingja to protect the travelers of Immortalis. The spirit is a Scandinavian personal protection spirit. When she saw how the people of Immortalis *all* needed protection, she became the road itself in sympathy for the citizens. As the road, she can protect everyone on it from malevolent spirits. Unfortunately, that is all the road will protect travelers from. Evil beings and beasts can still prey on unwary travelers. Although, many beasts avoid the road. They seem to be able to feel the spirit's presence, and avoid the road because of it.

A small trail leads off of the Hamingja road and spirals up the mountain to the city. It's at the top of this trail, this one full day trail that elevates a small amount of miles, that the city of Shambhala resides. From where Cap is at upon the trail he can see a small stream flowing from the town. This stream becomes a river as it flows west onto the plain. He remembers crossing the bridge where the river from the east and the river from the west collide. The turbulent water was ferocious when the two rivers met, then flowed to the south as one.

He can see magnificent Tibetan palaces and temples as they climb the ascent into the town. Shambhala is an unbelievably huge city on top of a large mountain. Cap cannot believe the size of the mountains. He can only compare them to the Himalayas, and those seem small in comparison. Surprisingly, the oxygen level here is no different than on the plains. He isn't out of breath, nor is his heart beating rapidly. Athena explained this to him. Immortalis is a land of plenty, and this included the air. It isn't thinner and it isn't less. It is a mythical and magical land, and not all the rules of physics apply. At least that's how Cap sees it.

Cap's reaction to seeing the town is completely awestruck. Unlike El Dorado, this city doesn't need to be made of gold to look well off. Just the architecture and its location alone are enough to make the most seasoned traveler stop and stare. As soon as he can get his eyes and mind back to the ground, he sees Athena's chariot take the lead. He follows the chariot to the largest palace in the city. He pulls up alongside of the chariot as it slows to a stop.

"Well, Sir Casey," Athena says, "You are in for a treat. Two of the world's greatest heroes are about to spar with each other."

"What?" Cap asks.

"See those two men circling?"

"Yeah."

"That is Cuchulain and Heracles."

"Oh," Cap's understanding begins to figure it out. The two men are equal in size and height. Heracles is dressed in Greek armor, with a lion fur robe. His skin is slightly tanner than his adversary, and his hair is a sandy brown color. His counterpart, Cuchulain, is dressed in Celtic attire. His skin is lighter, and his hair is red. The distance from which Cap is from them doesn't allow for distinctive features. He couldn't help but notice that the two could be confused with each other, except for their hair.

The two warriors rush each other, colliding with a thunderous sound. The two men's great strength vibrates into the ground, causing a small quake that shakes everything around. They wrestle for a few minutes, and then back off of each other when neither can get an advantage. They each pull out their weapons. Heracles is carrying his large olive-wood club. Cuchulain is holding the gae bolga. An inhumane spear, its broad head is barbed and set with narrow slits that hooks come out of when impaled into an enemy.

The two men circle each other again, deeply aware of the lethal weapon the other is holding. Cuchulain thrusts first, Heracles parrying the strike. The battle becomes a blur as both men begin moving too fast for the normal eye to see. The metallic clash of armor, the thud of the weapons clashing, and the occasional grunt are the only things that are discernible. Minutes pass as the growing crowd remains silent with anticipation, curious to see who will be the victor. Dust fills the air, blowing all around from the wind of their weapons. Thunder is heard as the heroes collide, throwing each other back. They stand in battle stance for a moment, and then simultaneously stand straight. They walk to each other, greeting and congratulating the other on their skills. All around Cap, the crowd begins to cheer and clap, very much entertained by the two heroes.

They walk side by side towards Cap and Athena. Neither of them looks tired, although they are breathing heavily. Cap is star struck as the two demigods get closer. Athena stands tall, very proud of the two men.

"Well done," she says, congratulating them both.

"Thank you, my lady," Cuchulain says gratefully, bowing to the goddess.

"Thanks sis," responds Heracles in between breaths.

"I would like to introduce you to Sir Casey," she says to them, lifting a hand towards Cap, "He is the commander of the Avalon forces. Sir Casey, this is Cuchulain and Heracles."

"It's an honor," Cap says to them.

The two men look him up and down, measuring him up. Heracles speaks to him first, "Sir Casey. I thought you would be bigger. You look small for the hero that stood up to the Vampiric Army."

"Agreed," says Cuchulain, "I must admit, from the stories I've heard, I expected someone much different."

Cap frowns, ashamed of his size in the presence of such great men. "I'm no hero," he tells them, "I just survived, that's all."

"But you *did* survive," Athena reassures him, "No commander who has faced up to the vampires has ever returned."

"You've become what no one has expected," Cuchulain adds.

"That is the true beginning of all heroes," Heracles informs.

"Thank you," Cap says gratefully, "but I still don't think I am a hero. Not compared to either one of you, anyways."

"We'll find out in time," Heracles says to him, implying something with his grin.

"I'm also curious to see also, Sir Casey," Cuchulain says, agreeing with his companion.

"Please, call me Cap," he says, "What is it you can't wait to see?"

The two men just laugh, which makes Cap more confused, and a little aggravated. Athena just remains silent for a moment, continuing to smile proudly. "Sir Casey," she says, "Go tour the palace. I'm sure you'd enjoy that. I have some private matters to discuss with Heracles and Cuchulain."

"I would. Thank you, my lady," he says to her. He turns to his men, "Take care of her. I shouldn't be long." He dismounts Pegasus, petting it softly on the nose, and walks into the palace, taking Adflictus with him.

Athena watches him until he is out of sight, then turns to the two heroes. "Don't tell me you plan on challenging him."

"I must know what he's capable of," says Heracles.

"There is something about him," Cuchulain tells her, "Something in his posture, or maybe in his eyes that gets the blood burning for battle."

"He's only human," Athena says, concerned.

"We know that. We aren't going to kill him," explains Heracles, almost laughing, "just see how he fares."

"When he loses? What then?" Athena asks.

"We will know where to place him in our forces," answers Cuchulain.

Concern continues to show in the goddess' eyes. Then an idea forms, and she smiles, "And if he wins?"

Heracles laughs hard, "It is impossible!"

Athena's smile doesn't fade, "Humor me."

Heracles tries to control his laughter as he speaks, "If he wins, my men and I will fall under Cap's command. How does that sound?"

Cuchulain laughs harder than Heracles, "Defeats both of us? I and all the Celt forces will fall under his command."

A male's voice echoes out from behind Athena, "The Norse army will also."

Athena turns around to see who spoke. "Odin?" she says, surprised to see the god.

"Athena, my dear. It has been far too long," he says.

Both Cuchulain and Heracles are stunned, speechless from surprise. Athena's surprise fades as her curiosity grows. "Why are you in Shambhala?" she asks him.

"Even we ruling gods need to travel the land from time to time. I find myself fortunate to be in the right place at the right time." he answers her.

Her face shows disbelief, "May I ask why you would offer the Norse forces though?"

Odin laughs, "If one mortal could come close to defeating two half god half man heroes, he's earned the right to command an army of thousands. I must admit though, I'd rather see a Norse hero commanding our forces. I'll wait to see if he wins or not."

Athena nods, agreeing with the god. She turns back to the two heroes, "Well now, it seems that the stakes have risen. I will agree to the challenge. I would like to see him in action as well."

Both men smile, pleased with the goddess. Around them, people begin to whisper amongst themselves. Soon, a few people leave the area to spread the news. It is to become a momentous day. Heracles AND Cuchulain are challenging the hero of Avalon. Such a thing has never occurred in the city, and the news spreads fast. Very soon, the area begins to get crowded with people. Everyone wanting to catch a glimpse, no one wanting to say they have missed it. As the crowd thickens, Cap's cavalry half circles around the gods and heroes, giving them both room and protection.

Out of nowhere, all of the leading gods of the land appear. Zeus of the Greeks, Lugh of the Celts, Re of the Egyptians. Zeus turns to Athena, "So, Hermes' message is true. This human will battle the two heroes."

Athena bows to him, "Yes, father. Heracles and Cuchulain wish to challenge him."

All the gods look at each other, nodding in a silent approval. Zeus looks around, contemplating, "Then all of the people in Immortalis should see this," he says.

Cap walks out of the palace, satisfied with his quick tour. His walk slows as the large crowd begins to cheer around him. His jaw drops, and he stops in the middle of the area. He looks around, confused and shocked by what is going on. The amount of people gathering is unbelievable, and their silence has suddenly gotten so quiet he thinks he can hear the mountain breathe. Heracles and Cuchulain walk out to him.

"We would like to spar with you, Cap," Heracles tells him.

"With me?" Cap asks confused, "but why?"

"It is just something we must do," Cuchulain explains.

Cap laughs out loud in response. "You want to spar with me? The two of you? Now that's funny. Seriously, what's going on?"

"Seriously," Cuchulain says to him, "We *are* challenging you."

Cap looks around the crowd. Everyone is silent as death, waiting for Cap's answer. "Doesn't look like much of a choice," he says, very unsure of himself, "Very well. I will spar with you."

The crowd cheers with a thunderous roar. The gods all nod with approval. They raise their open hands, and then a flash of white covers the area. When Cap regains his vision, he finds his back against the wall of a sandy arena. His men and Athena are in the seats behind him.

"What the-" he says out loud.

"You are in the City of Caesars' coliseum," Athena explains to him, "From here, the gods will project the fight all over Immortalis. Everyone will be allowed to witness this."

"That sounds like a lot considering it is just a sparring session," Cap says, looking around. The seats of the arena are full with people wanting to watch.

"Don't let it bother you," she assures him.

"Don't let it bother me," Cap says sarcastically, "Apparently, you gods and heroes are all comedians if you think the entire population of Immortalis watching *won't* bother me."

"The people need entertainment," she says in explanation to him, "Everyone needs to smile and cheer from time to time."

"I'll agree with that," he says wide eyed looking around, "but it sure doesn't help any." He takes a deep breath, trying to calm his nerves, "Alright. Let's do this before I change my mind and flee like a coward."

He begins walking out to the middle of the arena. Athena watches him, concerned. 'I hope he wins,' she thinks. That is all she can do. Maybe that is all he needs.

Heracles meets him in the center of the arena. "Are you ready?" he asks.

"Nope," Cap says, getting into a fighting stance, "but let's go!"

Heracles swings his club suddenly, Cap barely blocking the blow with his shield. The hit skids him back quite a ways, Heracles' immense strength showing. Heracles begins attacking immediately, pushing Cap backwards towards the wall. Cap just blocks and parries, trying to keep up with the increasing speed of the hero. The crowd cheers with excitement, but the two men cannot hear it. They are concentrating far too hard to notice.

Cap can feel the wall getting closer, and he worries that he might be forced to give up. Right then, Heracles changes strategies. Cap sees the opening and takes it. He begins striking and swinging as fast as he can. The advantage changes and Heracles is now getting backed up. He swings at Cap in an effort to suspend, or stop the attack. Cap ducks under it, counter attacking immediately. Heracles parries the attack just in time. Cap continues to attack, driving the demigod back.

Cuchulain moves in, anxious to spar with Cap before his energy is depleted. Gae bolga ready, he rushes in quickly. Cap sees him rushing out the corner of his eye.   He gets his shield up just in time to block Cuchulain's thrust.

The hit slides Cap back about ten feet. He regains his posture as his adversaries stand side by side in fighting stances. "Am I that much of a threat?" Cap asks, breathing quickly.

"The challenge was against both of us," Cuchulain says, "Besides, I can't just let you two have all the fun. I want a chance at you also."

"As you wish," Cap says disappointed, "Alright then, when you're ready."

Heracles and Cuchulain spread out slowly. Cap backs up, keeping them both within his vision. They attack immediately, using all their speed and strength against Cap. Cap parries, blocks, and dodges attacks as fast as he can. He is unable to counter attack either of them, and his energy is beginning to fade fast. Right then, it is there. It is an unknown feeling within him, just begging to be released.

Cap doesn't have time to think on it. With his energy depleting quickly, he releases the unknown feeling inside of him. His vision turns red. The heroes' attacks seem to slow down. He no longer feels pain, only fury. He fights back with speed and power, only matched by that of his adversaries.

The three men battle at speeds that even the gods have never seen before. Cap continues to let the feeling within energize and power him. He ducks a swing from Heracles, Cap swings Adflictus low to the ground. The hook catches the man's ankle, pulling him down. Cap blocks a thrust from Cuchulain and swings Adflictus' outer curve onto the Heracles' chest.

"Dead," Cap says twisting Adflictus around so the point is laying atop the hero's chest. The crowd roars, shaking the ground as Cuchulain and Cap continue to battle. Heracles picks himself up and walks to the wall, staying out of the way.

The two men stand their ground, fighting in the center of the arena. Neither backs from their position. They strike and parry each other's attacks. Metal hits metal as the weapons continuously meet, causing sparks to fly. They fight without thinking, allowing instinct to guide their movements.

Cuchulain pulls back and thrusts the gae bolga as Cap swings the mace of Adflictus. The heads of the two weapons meet, creating a lightning flash and deafening thunder. The gae bolga slips through the hands of Cuchulain, hitting him unexpectedly in the stomach. The blow knocks the wind out of him, and drops him to his knees.

The spike of Adflictus is at Cuchulain's throat immediately. "Yield?" Cap asks. Cuchulain looks up at the man. He thinks of trying to get out of the situation, but he can see the fire burning within Cap's eyes. It is a fire that won't show more mercy than he's giving already. "Yield," Cap says again.

Cuchulain closes his eyes as his hand moves upward slowly. "I yield," he says as he pushes the spike away from his throat. The people cheer thunderously. A full human just defeated two of the land's greatest demigods!

Cap's vision goes back to normal, and he falls to his knees. The feeling that over took him exhausted everything within him. He is physically, mentally, and emotionally exhausted. He looks up and around. The crowd is on their feet, cheering for him. He's shocked as he can hear his nickname chanted throughout the arena. "CAP! CAP! CAP!" he hears over and over again. Cuchulain and Heracles stand over him as he soaks the cool evening air into his burning lungs.

"Can you walk?" Heracles asks as Cap forces himself up.

"Yeah, I think so," Cap replies, breathing very heavily.

"Good," says Cuchulain with a tired breath, "It will look better for the people if you walk out on your own. Follow us. We'll get you out of view quickly."

"Ok," is all Cap says to him.

The three men walk to the closest tunnel, entering it and getting out of the crowds view. The crowd's cheers are deafening within the tunnel. It is only till Cap is sure no one can see him that he stops and falls to his knees again, trying to catch his breath. Cuchulain and Heracles stand beside him, watching to make sure he is alright.

Athena appears in the tunnel, walking up to them. "It appears I am going to have to start calling you Cap," she says with a smile.

"And that's all I had to do for that?" Cap says humorously between breaths, "And I thought I would have to do something really stupid, like spar with two demigods, to impress you just so you would call me that."

"I just want to know," Heracles interrupts, "How did you do it? You fought like YOU are the demigod!"

"Agreed," Cuchulain adds, "You were able to keep up with me even after I used every bit of my battle spasm. How were you able to match us?"

"I don't know," Cap says, confused about it himself, "I honestly do not know."

Chapter 13

Heracles and Cuchulain guard the door of Cap's room. He's been unable to move for two days since sparring with the two heroes. Athena has visited him frequently. He found out about the wager from her. At first he was shocked and appalled, but then proud that she believed in him so much. He still had to mention that the safe bet would have been on the heroes, but her only response to that was then she would have lost.

He thinks about that as he forces himself to sit up, wincing at the pain in his back and abs. He looks at the door, considering getting up and leaving the room. He smiles, thinking of how Heracles and Cuchulain would act if he just walked out. They might be surprised. He's been bedridden for so long. They wouldn't suspect it. He decides to. He wants to see this city, the City of Caesars.

He tries to stand up, only to fall back on the bed with pain. He curses under his breath, sits up slowly, and tries to stand again. This time he keeps his balance. He gets dressed slowly, his muscles tender, and so stiff that they feel like dead wood. He debates on taking his shield and Adflictus. He looks at the door again, and not seeing a lock puts his shield on his left arm and grabs Adflictus. He walks slowly to the door, trying to loosen his muscles.

He walks out of the room. "Gentlemen," he says, greeting the two men with a smile.

"You're up," says Heracles, "That's good to see."

"Thank you," Cap responds.

"Is there anything you would like?" Cuchulain asks.

"I'd like to see the city," Cap answers, "Would you care to join me?"

"We'd be honored," Cuchulain answers.

"Great!" Cap exclaims, "But, could we go slow? I'm still not moving to well."

They both laugh hard. Cap turns red. Both embarrassed and irritated at having to show the weakness in front of them. They begin to leave the building, when a woman appears out of nowhere. She's a tall, gorgeous, brunette beauty. Cap thought that Athena was the most beautiful woman. This woman dwarfs that beauty by a country mile. There is nothing visual about her that isn't attractive. She wears a toga like Athena's, except that it is pink with shades of purple.

"Cap?" She asks inquiringly.

"Yes," he says, tightening his grip on Adflictus. He is suddenly cautious of the situation.

"I am Aphrodite," she says proudly, "I wanted to congratulate you personally for your successes."

"I thank you," he says.

"I also come bearing a gift from the Caesars as well," she says, pulling something from behind her back. It is a domed helmet with a neck guard in the back, with side face shields that go down to the jawbone. Two bars across the forehead area are riveted onto the helmet. A twist on crest holder was on top of the helmet, with very light orange feathers standing horizontally across the crest. It also has a carrying handle, and is a magnificent gold color, and extremely shiny. "It is made of orichalcum, the gold-copper alloy that is second only in value to pure gold. The Caesars feel that you need a helmet worthy of your new rank."

"My new rank?" he asks surprised.

"They didn't tell you?" she asks in response. Cap shakes his head no. "With Heracles', Cuchulain's, and the Norse forces now under your command, all the Caesars have voted unanimously to give you the rank of general. Do you accept there gift?"

"I'm honored to accept the gift of the Caesars. I find it admirable that the Caesars have so much confidence in me." he says.

She hands him the helmet, and he takes it from her with both hands. "Put it on," she tells him, "I would like to see it on you."

He does as she asks. Although the helmet is made of metal, Cap finds it very comfortable. He looks at Heracles and Cuchulain, and they both nod with approval. He turns his attention to Aphrodite. She seems to be looking at him with approval and admiration in her eyes. Yet, he can't help but feel uncomfortable in her presence. He senses something else. He doesn't know what it is, but he continues to be cautious.

"I would also like to discuss something with you. Would you be interested?" she asks him.

He looks at her warily, "That would depend on the subject."

"Could you give us a moment, gentlemen?" she asks Heracles and Cuchulain. They both bow and walk down the hallway, out of hearing distance. Aphrodite waits until she's sure they are far enough. "Relax," she tells Cap, "you seem far too tense. No one here will harm you."

"I'll be fine," he tells her, "What is it you would like to talk to me about?"

"I was wondering if a god, or goddess, with their abilities joining you would be helpful."

"It couldn't hurt," he answers

"Good! I would like to be that goddess."

Cap looks at her, unsure. "And you would be the only deity that would help me? I'm confused. I thought all the gods would be willing to help?"

"Many are," she answers, "but many won't be able to. Others won't be able to help all the time. I'm talking about being there for you, no matter what."

Cap is still confused. "So that's it?" he asks, "You just want to offer me your services?"

"Yes, but it's not that simple," she says, noticing the look of understanding coming to his face, "I would need something in return."

'There's always a catch,' he thinks to himself. "And what would that be?" he asks.

"I would need you to swear fealty to me."

"No," he says immediately.

"Now don't answer so fast. Take some time to think about it. With a god at your side, we could annihilate the enemy's forces. We would be the most powerful beings in Immortalis! I am willing to reward you," she leans in close to him, "reward you very, very well."

"Tempting," Cap says, "but it's still-"

"Don't answer yet," she interrupts, "It would be most beneficial for you to join me. I could make your life heaven here."

"And if I refuse?"

"I can also make your life a living hell," she answers with a sinister grin. She waits while Cap remains silent.

Cap considers the consequences of her proposal. Having a well-known goddess behind him in battle would be beneficial. He would lose any and all free choices, having to ask permission for just about everything. He also considers the far future. Would the war end? If it did, would there be another? Then and there he remembers what happens to men with too much power. "Yeah," he says meditatively, "I still say no."

"I beg you to reconsider," she says sternly, "The consequences could be devastating for you."

"Listen sister," he says irritated, his voice beginning to get louder with frustration, "This is the first war I've ever been in. As far as I know, you never had to watch men die because they believed and fought for you.

Not their kings, not their gods. I could be wrong, but the feeling is new to me. So excuse me if I'm a little agitated with all of this.

"I have a brother whose only goal is to kill me. I have no family! The only friends I have are the few I've made here, and most of them are in El Dorado! I have no home. I have no place to go to once this is all over! The only livelihood I'm likely to know here is war, and that's the pain and torture *I am offered!*

"I am destined to die for a land that is not my own, and watch men and women die horrible deaths beside me! I already know this! Now, tell me! How in the *hell* could you *possibly* make my life more of a hell than it already is!"

Cap looks at Aphrodite as she stands silent in shock. "Anything else?" he asks her. He waits a second as the shock of his yelling keeps her quiet, "Good." He begins walking towards Cuchulain and Heracles, but stops beside the goddess, speaking quietly to her, "I know where my loyalties and beliefs lie. Don't you *ever* question it," and walks away.

Cuchulain and Heracles are waiting for him with looks of concern on their faces. "Is everything alright?" Cuchulain asks.

"Nothing a bottle of whiskey can't fix," Cap answers, anger and irritation quivering his voice, "Let's go." They walk down the hallway, and towards the exit of the building.

Athena is walking up to the palace that Cap is staying in. She sees the trio leave the building and walk down the street in the opposite direction. She smiles at first, happy to see that Cap is up and moving around. She notices the helmet he's now wearing, liking the way it looks upon him. Her smile fades quickly as she sees how angry and aggravated he looks.

She stops in front of the palace door. She just stands there, watching them walk down the street. She can't help but wonder what would upset him so much. Aphrodite walks out, the look of shock still upon her face, but anger also.

"Aphrodite," Athena greets her, "What brings you to the city?"

"He's a fool," she says angrily, not acknowledging the question.

"What?" Aphrodite asks.

"I've offered my services to him," she says, talking to herself more than to Athena, "I offered him rewards. I only asked for his loyalty in return. He declined, and spoke to me like no mortal ever has before."

"What are you talking about?" Athena asks more eagerly.

Aphrodite speaks with confusion and anger, "I thought that if a god or goddess would be behind Cap in his battles, the war could end quickly. He didn't disagree. But when I asked for his fealty in return, he declined and got angry. Then he yelled at me in anger. I'd punish him, but there doesn't seem to be anything he's afraid of. I can't believe my charms didn't work! I must punish him! No one talks to a goddess like that. No one talks to *me* like that! No one!"

Athena holds back her laughter. "Calm down," she tells her, "Cap is persistent, and stubborn. He's been handed a full plate, and he hasn't had time to digest it all yet. I think he's doing very well, considering the situation. He's not from here, and he's been thrown into a web of disaster that he never wanted to be in. But he has a good heart, and cares for others. He will do what he thinks is best. All we can do is support him, and help him whenever we can."

"It is not enough," Aphrodite says to her, "He should have been more than willing!"

"Who can know what a mortal is thinking," Athena reassures her, "I'm sure he has his reasons for declining."

"They had better be good."

"I would think so."

Aphrodite wouldn't say anything more. She just keeps her face stern, and walks away. Athena turns around, heading towards the archive building. All the ruling gods agreed to look into Cap's family lineage, wanting to know his bloodline. After watching him take on Heracles and Cuchulain, she is curious also. What he did seemed impossible, yet he did it. There has to be an answer somewhere. She enters to see all the muses and nymphs buried in books and scrolls.

"Have you found anything?" she asks them.

"We've traced his bloodline back on his mother's side," one of the muses answers.

"And?" Athena asks, growing impatient.

"He's a grandson of Cuchulain," the muse tells her.

'That means he's a grandson of Lugh!' she thinks to herself. "Are you certain?" she asks them, "Cuchulain's son was killed in battle."

They all nod their heads completely certain of their findings. "Not before his son fathered a child himself," the muse says.

She turns to a group of nymphs. "Have you fared as well?" she asks them.

"We've been searching non-stop for two days," one of the nymphs tells her, "We've traced his paternal ancestors back to Heracles, but we just found it. We are double checking it right now."

'That ties him to both Zeus and Lugh!' she thinks to herself, 'He defeated his own ancestors in battle!'

"How is this possible?" she thinks out loud, not meaning to.

"Many millennia have passed between the heroes and Cap," a muse tells her, "Both Heracles and Cuchulain had children. We've traced his lineage throughout all of Europe, parts of Asia and Egypt. It is possible that he could be related to other heroes and gods as well. It was only a matter of time before the descendants of demigods came together in one person."

Well, Heracles has enormous strength and cunningness. Cuchulain has the battle spasms that increase his speed, strength, and lethality. It is possible those traits could have passed down dormant through the generations. With thousands of years in between, anything is possible.

Aphrodite storms into the archives suddenly, making them all jump. "Tell me about Cap's brother. I need to know about his brother!"

One of the nymphs bows down to her, "My lady. It appears that they are adopted brothers. His brother was adopted before Cap was born. We are currently searching for his bloodline."

"So they don't have the same ancestry?" Athena asks.

"No, not at all," the nymph answers.

"Keep looking," she tells the nymphs and muses. She turns to Aphrodite, "I have to tell Hermes about all of this. He needs to relate all this to New Olympus." Athena turns and runs out of the building, and towards the bathhouses. Hermes is there, or she had heard earlier. She runs through the streets, dodging people as she passes them. The thoughts rushing through her head just as fast as she is running. She bursts into the bathhouse, disregarding all others. She almost falls into the bath Hermes is in, and begins talking faster than he can understand.

"Excuse me!" he yells at her.

"Oh, cover it up!" she yells back, "This is too important to wait!"

"What?" he asks, placing a white towel over himself, "And slow down so I can understand you. You're talking so fast, you sound like a Roman."

She closes her eyes and takes a deep breath. She then calmly tells Hermes everything about Cap and his heritage. Everything to her knowledge. From the history that Cap had told her, and what the nymphs and muses had related to her. Hermes has to slow her down from time to time, but she continues her message. When she finishes, she just stands there breathing very hard. She just stares at him, "Well?" she says, trying to hurry him.

"I'll deliver the message right away," he tells her, "As soon as you leave me be to get dressed."

"Of course," she says, suddenly turning red with embarrassment. She turns and leaves the bathhouse.

Chapter 14

Cap looks over his men, greeting and talking to as many as he possibly can. They still look weary from their journey to Shambhala, but their spirits are up. After watching him spar with Cuchulain and Heracles, they're moral is very high. Although Cap doesn't agree with it, they hold him in a higher regard then they have before. It is something that didn't seem possible after Avalon, but he is constantly being surprised by everything in this land anymore. He also talks to each one with great admiration. Even though they fight for him, he allows them to make their own choices. The choice all of them have made was to fight with him. Just that alone deserves his admiration and trust.

After talking to the last of his men, he takes a walk around their camp. A makeshift corral is set up for the horses. The grass within it is more than enough for all of the horses. He can see Pegasus in the corral, eating and playing with the other horses. As he walks up to the corral, Pegasus notices him and trots over.

"Looks like you're having fun," he says softly to the winged horse. Pegasus snorts as an answer. Cap pets him lightly on the nose, then watches as he goes back to playing with the other horses.

"I think you're getting attached," Heracles says to him.

"Yeah, I know," Cap responds, "It'll hurt when he leaves. I know."

"You can't know that," Cuchulain says incredulously.

"I can," Cap says with sorrow, "He is a free spirit. He will leave when he is ready."

Both heroes look at each other, but remain silent as Cap turns around, looking at the mountains that the city is located between. The mountain to the north is made of gold, the one to the south of diamonds. Cap just stares, unaware that he is being watched. He just bathes in the sunlight, and the beautiful reflection off of the mountains. He brings his head back down, knowing he needs to be in reality.

"So what do you think his next move will be?" Cuchulain asks.

"Don't you mean her?" Cap asks in return.

"No. I mean Cronus," answers Cuchulain.

"Cronus? The titan?" Cap asks confused, "I thought Breanna was the leader of the enemy forces?"

"No one has told you yet?" Heracles asks.

"Apparently not," Cap answers.

"Well," Cuchulain says with a small smile, "it looks like our young general needs an education."

"Enough of the jokes," says Cap, aggravated, "fill me in. Tell me what's going on."

"Alright," replies Heracles, "the short version is that Cronus is still upset for being defeated by Zeus, and is willing to destroy everything for revenge."

"And another piece is added to the game," Cap says disappointed.

"Huh? What do you mean?" Cuchulain asks.

"Chess, but never mind the game," Cap says, "I thought it was supposed to be a commander battle between me and Breanna, or Breanna and Luke," Cap says.

"Sorry," is all Heracles says.

"Great! Just fricken great!" Cap exclaims sarcastically, "What's next? Do I have to walk on water to make peace? How about flying? Do I need to take a flying leap off of a tall cliff? Would that work? Argh!"

"Calm down," Cuchulain says, recognizing the look in Cap's eyes, "We thought you knew."

"I'm not mad," Cap says taking deep breaths, "It's just getting to be too much to digest. Zombies, vampires, werecats, werewolves, heroes, titans, and gods all packaged together in a fight to the death. Somewhere in between, regular humans are mixed in. And, let's not forget, by some mistake of nature, my brother and me in a mortal battle as well. Excuse me for getting upset, but it is frustrating!"

Athena's voice rings out from behind him, "Is everything alright?"

Cap turns around and bows to the goddess, "Just fine, Athena. Apparently, everything seems to be right in place."

Athena looks at him concerned. "You don't sound to convincing," she says.

"Everything's fine," he says. He turns so he can look at all three of them. "If you would please excuse me, I need a moment to collect my thoughts, and attempt to plan ahead." Cap turns and walks away.

The three watch as Cap takes himself out of their view. Athena gives a stern look at the two heroes, "Do I dare ask?"

"He just found out about Cronus," Heracles states.

"He wasn't too happy about it," adds Cuchulain.

"I can see that," Athena says, "I just assumed that he knew."

They all get silent. Each lost in thought, each worried about Cap in their own way. None of them notice Aphrodite running up to them. Not one of them notices the eyes in hiding staring at them. Aphrodite almost runs into all of them before she even notices them standing there.

"Where's Cap?" she asks.

"He's taking a moment," Athena answers.

"I need to see him," Aphrodite says, "I want to amend my offer to him."

"I don't think now would be such a good time," Cuchulain tells her.

"With how he's feeling, he might take it as an insult," adds Heracles.

Aphrodite doesn't say anything, but looks to be thinking about something. There's a shuffling behind a bush. No one notices until Cap comes out from behind it, dragging a young girl with him.

"Found us a little spy," he says.

"I'm not a spy!" the kid exclaims, trying to break free of Cap's grip.

"You want to explain why you were hiding in the bushes?" Cap asks.

"I've got news for Sir Casey," she says, "Do you know where he is?"

"I'm Sir Casey," Cap states.

"Ok," she says, ceasing her struggle, "I have news for you from El Dorado."

"What?" Cap asks confused, "How did you know I was here? Better yet, how did you get here?"

"I convinced a griffin to give me a ride," she explains.

"Huh?" Cap asks, still confused, "You're not human, are you?"

"Of course not!" the girl says, "I'm an Akka." She waits as Cap racks his brain to think what an Akka is. Impatient, she speaks again, "I'm a Finnish goddess. And you're supposed to be smart!"

"Yeah, yeah," Cap says unamused, letting her go, "What's the news?"

She takes a deep breath, "El Dorado has been under siege since you left. It fell last night. Your friends have been captured. The woman called Breanna was debating on torturing them or not."

"How do you know all of this?" Athena asks her.

"I'm an unknown goddess that looks like a child. It is very easy for me to slip away without notice," she says, "My message is delivered. I'll leave now." She leaves, not waiting for any more questions.

Thoughts of pain and fear for Cap's friends enter his mind. Everyone remains silent, but anyone could tell that they were thinking the same things. The enemy has changed their tactics. What could they do now? With one message, the entire view of the world had changed. Now, not one person could be sure of the future. The only thing that seems for certain is a lot of pain, and death.

Cap looks up, and speaks to his companions, "I have to go." He turns around, heading back to the corral. "Pegasus!" he calls out. The pterippus trots up to him. "Would you take me back to El Dorado?" he asks. The horse paws at the ground, and shakes its head up and down in answer. "Great!" he says, "I'll get the saddle." He turns and heads over to the side of the corral where the saddles are kept. Aphrodite comes running up to him.

"You can't go!" she tells him.

"I have to," he answers, picking up the saddle and walking back to Pegasus.

"You can't do it on your own," Athena pleads with him, "Give us some time to get some forces together to go with you."

"No time," he replies to her.

"If you don't give us time to prepare the armies, we can't help you," Cuchulain explains.

"I'm not asking you to," Cap tells him, placing the saddle upon Pegasus' back.

"You'll need help," Heracles says, "We just need a little time."

"There is no time," Cap responds, "They don't have any time at all."

"But it is suicide!" exclaims Aphrodite, "If you go alone, you could be captured. Or worse!"

"Look," Cap says tightening the cinch, "it's something I have to do. Please, just try to understand that."

"We can help. Let us help you," Aphrodite pleads, "It could be a trap."

"It very well could be," Cap says, getting irritated as he climbs into the saddle, "Listen, if you all want to help, do this. Heracles and Cuchulain can ready the armies and meet me at El Dorado. I assume you two can get there faster than if you would follow the Hamingja road, right?" They both nod their heads. "Good, you will know what to do when you get there. As for you two," he says to Aphrodite and Athena, "Just do what you can. I'm not sure what the two of you combined are capable of, but I'm sure it is something great."

"But, why must you go alone?" asks Aphrodite.

"Because they are my friends. They need help. I can't sit by and wait. I know what I should do, but this is what I *have* to do. They are the closest friends I have right now. No offense meant. It's not a choice for me, I have to help them." He talks softly so that only Aphrodite can hear, "This is why I won't swear fealty to anyone. Things like this cannot require permission," he explains. "Let's go!" he tells Pegasus. The flying horse leaps into the air, does a quick circle, and flies quickly to the west.

The group stares into the sky. The reflection of the sun on his armor and Pegasus make the flying pair seem to glow. They continue watching until they are no longer in sight. King Arthur walks up to them as the shock of his sudden departure begins to wear off of them.

"Is Cap around?" King Arthur asks, "I'm hoping to discuss a few things with him."

"He just left for El Dorado, alone," Aphrodite tells him.

"But, I had heard it was under siege!" the king exclaims.

"So it is," says Heracles, "He left to save his friends. We need to leave immediately. Cuchulain, could you get Cap's men and meet me where our armies are camped?"

"I will," Cuchulain answers.

"You are going to help him?" King Arthur asks.

"How can we not," Cuchulain says, "The man is walking into certain death just to give aid to his friends. Any one of us would do the same."

"Give me a moment," the king says to them, "The knights have just arrived this morning. I will have them join you."

"I'm going too," Athena says.

"Me too," adds Aphrodite.

King Arthur watches as they all go their separate ways to prepare. He watches with both amusement and admiration. Gods and heroes are taking themselves into harm's way, his own knights included. He knows that Sir Palomedes won't hesitate to take up arms and dive into a fight to help Cap. All of them are going into harm's way to help a normal, mortal being. He must have all of their faith and friendship, along with their greatest respect.

He can't help but smile. They all believe in him that much. So much in fact, that armies are willingly marching to save a man who is knowingly walking into the teeth of death. Gods are rushing to aid this mortal man. Friends out to help a friend. A friend who is out to help his friends in mortal danger. It is very poetic.

Chapter 15

Day fades into night as the ceremony begins. No one can tell in the windowless room though. Logan, Adolf, and Diamondback watch with hatred and anger in their eyes. Chained to chairs against the wall, they are involuntarily forced to be witnesses to this succession of power. It is a double edged sword for Breanna. The elders, tricked into peace, and then humbled by forcefully and unwillingly relinquishing power to a much younger person. A much younger woman. Breanna and her new governor will now control Avalon and El Dorado, including all the surrounding areas.

Isabella looks absolutely stunning and proud as she waits patiently for Breanna to officially name her governor. She tries not to smile, remembering how Breanna used the elders' greed against them. The old men only think about gold and monetary values. So, after five days of the siege, they willingly met with the vampire after her threats of melting the town to the ground. In the treaty she offered that the town would remain standing, that their lives would be spared, and that it will truly become the richest town in all of Immortalis. Only if they swore fealty to her and Cronus though. They had no idea that she would take their governing positions away from them.

Isabella looks around the room. All around her are vampires, imps, and werecats. The only humans in the room are the elders, Luke, Logan, Diamondback, and herself. In all truthfulness though, it is only her, Logan and the elders. Luke is turning into a were-being. His hair is getting longer and much darker. Diamondback is immune to all venoms and poisons, making him something more than human. She looks over to the three men chained to the wall. She feels pity for them, not knowing what their fate will be.

Her attention is brought back to the ceremony as Breanna speaks her name. Her heart begins to beat rapidly as she waits for the moment. It has taken years, and she's had to beg, borrow and steal just to get an audience with the vampire. She was just shy of selling her soul to get what she wanted. Here it is now, the moment she's been working for her entire life. The moment everyone had told her was impossible to achieve.

Breanna turns from the audience to speak to her. "Isabella, please kneel," she tells her. Isabella kneels down, bowing her head. Breanna continues speaking, "It is with great honor and gratitude that I award you this high position. You have worked hard, and sacrificed much," she places a gold medallion on a silver necklace around her neck. A panther's face surrounded by bluebell flowers is engraved on it. "With great sacrifice and determination, you have earned this," Breanna says to her, "You were Isabella, the servant. Now rise, Governor Isabella."

Isabella stands up and all in the room applaud, very formally. Her face glows with pride, and her blood races in anticipation to get started. Unfortunately, she's forced to wait. She stands in her place, thanking each vampire, werecat, and imp that congratulates her. Finally, after what feels like forever, Breanna's subordinates leave the room. All but Salma, Martine, and Luke. The three prisoners remain restrained.

"Now it is time for business," Breanna tells everyone.

"What's first?" Isabella asks, anxious to begin.

"You need to gather what's left of your soldiers. I need at least half of them," she says.

Isabella's face turns grim, "You need half of them? For what?"

Breanna looks at her with disbelief that she would question her, "This deal was made that you would serve us. Not to question me."

Diamondback yells from where he sits, "You traitorous-"

"Diamondback!" Logan stops him, "Not now."

"These are my people now," Isabella complains, "I will need them all for defense once they find out about this. They will attack!"

"The defense of El Dorado is your concern, the campaign of Immortalis is mine," Breanna says, backing Isabella into the wall, "I want half. You'll give me half. No if's, and's, or but's!"

"Yes, Madame," Isabella says quietly, anger showing in her eyes.

"Good," Breanna tells her, "Volunteers would be nice. They will be more cooperative, but by force will be just as good."

"Of course," Isabella says, still holding in her anger.

"Next," Breanna orders, looking around the room.

"We need to discuss the next directive in our plan of attack," Salma says.

Breanna gets a thoughtful look on her face, "If I understood Cronus right, we will follow the river south, towards Elysian Fields."

"That will be fun," chuckles Martine, smiling at the thoughts in her head.

"Are we ready for that?" Salma asks, "That's the home of heroes. A lot of heroes. Do you think we have enough numbers in our army for that?"

"I do," Breanna answers, "In a couple of days, our forces will be tripled. All of the vampire clans will arrive. No army will be able to stand up to that," she turns to Martine, "How many werecats will we have?"

"My entire pride, plus all of the other five prides. There should be a thousand or more. They should arrive shortly after your vampires," Martine tells her.

"Great!" Breanna exclaims, "With all the zombies we do have and will have, plus what we can get on the way, our army will be in the tens of thousands."

"And the Leviathan," Luke adds.

Breanna looks at Salma, "Do you still wonder if we will have enough?"

"I'm still skeptical," Salma answers, "I think we should prepare for problems."

"What problems could possibly happen?" Luke asks her, "This sounds fool proof!"

"But there's always factors that get in the way," she tells him.

"Like what?" he asks, "My brother? He's just one person. How much harm could he possibly do?"

"By himself," Breanna says, "probably little. But if he has a force behind him, possibly a lot. He's already shown that he has a good ability to command."

"So what do we do about him?" Martine asks. Everyone in the room remains silent in thought, not quite sure of what to do. Ideas flow through their heads, but no one says any of them out loud. They need something that has no chance for failure. Something that would incapacitate him for a long while.

Luke looks around the room, his eyes stopping on the three prisoners. "What about them?" he asks.

"They," Breanna says, pointing to them, "they fought bravely and honorably. They also fight under Cap. They get the choice of death or joining us."

"Death," Adolf says, "I won't join a group of demons."

"You might get your wish," Martine says, "Filthy werewolf!"

"He won't get a choice," Breanna says pointing at Logan, "Especially that one. He won't be able to resist."

"Try it," Diamondback says angrily, "I dare you to. Just let me out of these chains when you do. See what happens."

"I was thinking bait," Luke says.

"What do you mean?" Salma asks, "Explain yourself."

"Cap has always held his friends in high regard," Luke tells them, "Use them as bait. Lure him away from us. Have Isabella hold them hostage. He will come for them. Even with an army, he will waste time trying to save them. If he's forced to waste days here, it'll make him behind us in as many days. He'll never catch up!"

"I'll think about it," Breanna says, "it might work. But come, we have work that needs done before dawn. Isabella, I want those men in front of me before daylight."

"Yes, Madame," Isabella answers quietly. She waits patiently as they leave the room. After they all have left, she goes to the door and calls Captain Gonzales in.

"You asked for me, governor?" he asks with disgust.

"Yes," she replies, "Breanna wants half of our forces. We are to give them to her before daybreak."

His look of disgust turns into a look of shock. "Half!" he exclaims.

"We're not giving it to her," she tells him, "At least, not what she thinks she'll get. She doesn't know our total number of soldiers, not soldiers and militia. Give her the weakest and wounded. She never said what shape they had to be in."

"With all due respect, I don't want to give her a single soul," he protests.

"Either do I. I just haven't figured out to get out of this yet. We either give them to her, or she will take them by force. I'd like to keep as many here as possible. We may need all of them real soon." she explains.

"What do you know that I don't?" the captain asks.

"Let me answer that for you," Logan says from across the room, "They're thinking of keeping us caged and used as bait. They're hoping it buys time for them to move on down the road."

"You're going to sacrifice us to help them?" the captain half exclaims, half asks Isabella.

"Not if I don't have to," she says.

"May I speak openly, governor?"

"Of course, captain."

"Why did you do it? You've taken away our freedom and forced us into servitude!"

"Because I was always told I couldn't," she answers, "I was just a little servant girl, and nothing more. I wanted to do more. I wanted to do something great." His face remains confused, so she continues, "How I did it may be wrong, but the elders are out of the way. They held us back more than anything. Particularly me. They would have killed us all just to save their 'precious' gold."

"I don't understand," he says.

"I'll explain later," she tells him, "Go. Find the men we will be giving to her." He bows to her, speechless, and walks out of the room. She takes in a large sigh. Her plans have changed in only a matter of minutes. At this point, she's beginning to question whether her quest for power was the right decision or not. She thought that Breanna and Cronus would make her governor, and then leave her and the town alone. She knew she would have to serve. She never considered that she would have to force the rest of the town to service also. She is going to have to make this right somehow, someway. Only, she doesn't know how. In what possible way would she be able to make this right?

"So that's what this was all about?" Diamondback asks, taking her out of her trance, "Your personal quest for power? You are endangering lives and livelihoods for nothing but a title!"

She hangs her head, ashamed. "I didn't mean for all of this," she says to herself more than him, "We've always been isolated and neutral. I never believed that they would demand so much."

"So, do something about it," he tells her.

"What could I possibly do?" she asks, tears beginning to form in her eyes, "I swore fealty. Now, I'm just a servant with a title."

Adolf looks her in the eye, "We determine our own destinies with our choices. The only difference now is that your choices will affect others far more drastically."

"I never thought of it that way," she says, "I'm not sure that I was ever ready."

"So you made a deal with the devil," Logan says to her, "Are you gonna make that your life? What's the worst that could happen?"

"They will kill me, and destroy the town," she answers, sobbing.

"And that's what worries you?" Adolf asks.

"Yes," she says.

Diamondback begins laughing. "Let me tell you something," he says, "Immortality isn't living forever, and it isn't about life. Life is what you make of it. Long, or short, it is good because we make it good, and bad because we let it get that way. Immortality, true immortality, is being remembered forever. Those remembered the most have been either great in some way, or terrible and evil. How you will be remembered is up to you."

She looks at him disbelief, "You make it sound simple."

"Well, it's not difficult," he responds.

She leans against the wall, contemplating everything. Everything is out of order. Nothing is the way she had planned. Now, instead of living a life of luxury and power, she's living in powerless despair. It feels like all hope is lost, but according to her prisoners, she can change everything. She smiles at the thought, its comfort surrounding her. Although, she has no idea where to start.

She brushes the tears from her face, and stands up proudly. If she can change things, then she will change them. What she needs is a start, a catalyst, just something. Preferably something small. That way it would be harder to detect, possibly unnoticed completely. That would be ideal. She tries to think of something that could get her out of this predicament, but nothing comes to mind. She feels disappointment, knowing that she will be forced to wait.

She looks at the three men restrained in front of her. A thought of setting them free enters her mind, but she discards it. Setting them free with Breanna still in town would be ridiculous. She'd kill them immediately! The thought of sending them to their deaths sends shivers down her spine. 'Something else,' she thinks, 'There has to be something else.'

A commotion outside the room turns her head. She can hear people running and jumping, along with shrieks of fright. At first, she thinks the worst. It only takes a few moments for her to find out what the commotion is. Under the door, two snakes slither into the room. A western diamondback rattlesnake, its tan body with its diamond pattern on its back, and black stripes just before its rattles on its tail slithers towards Diamondback. Right behind it follows a black mamba. The snake is brownish grey in color, with a coffin shaped head. Being ten feet in length, it takes a few moments for the snake to clear the door. Isabella jumps against the wall, surprised and scared at the sudden appearance of the two venomous snakes.

"Stressly! Aminah!" exclaims Diamondback, "What took you so long?" Both snakes hiss in response, or what seems to be a response. Diamondback gets a look of confusion across his face. "Interesting," he says as they slither under his chair, and coil up.

Isabella moves slowly away from the wall. Her curiosity taking over her fear. "You-you can understand them?" she asks.

"Yes, I can," Diamondback answers.

"What do they say?"

"Whatever is on their mind," he answers, "Right now, they've informed me that they have been forced to hide. They're venom doesn't affect the zombies. Which only makes sense. They are dead, being controlled only by magic. It does have an effect on the vampires though. It doesn't kill them, but it does bring them down to earth." he laughs, " In a matter of speaking."

A pounding on the door interrupts them. "Governor Isabella," a females voice calls out, "snakes have been spotted around here. Let us know if you see them. We've found someone who's willing to kill them."

Isabella looks over at Diamondback and the two snakes. Diamondback's face remains stern, but his eyes show fear. She turns back towards the door, "Thank you," she calls out to the person, "I will let someone know if I see any." Diamondback breathes a sigh of relief as they here footsteps leave the doorway. The moment only lasts a moment though, as someone knocks on the door yet again.

"Governor?" Captain Gonzales' voice echoes through the room as he walks in. "I've assembled the men, and they will be waiting for Breanna in the morning. There is some-" he stops as he sees the two snakes.

He is about to call out when Isabella stops him, "Stop!" she orders, "What is it you were saying?"

He continues, his eyes never leaving the snakes. "There is something very odd with the weather," he says nervously, "It appears that a large thunderstorm is headed our way."

"What's odd about that?" she asks, "It has been storming since the siege began, and it hasn't let up."

"This is bigger," he says, "and it is coming from the east."

"What?" she asks in disbelief, "I have to see this. Stay here. Don't let anyone in except for me. Understand?"

"Yes, governor," he answers.

Isabella leaves the room, and out of the building. She steps out into a cold, light rain. Above her in the sky, sheet lightning flashes across the sky, and soft thunder rolls throughout the town. She pays it no mind, running to the east gate. Taking the steps to the rampart atop the wall, she finds that she's joining Martine and Luke.

Looking to the east, she sees what Captain Gonzales was talking about. Thunderclouds, larger than she has ever seen, appear on the horizon as it pushes the storm above her back to the west. Vampires all around begin scrabbling for cover as the afternoon daylight begins to shine between the storms. Fork lightning strikes ferociously and continuously, appearing to be angry with the ground itself. It only seems like seconds pass, then a deafening thunder. She places her hands over her ears as the sound rolls by. Never before has thunder sounded that loud, at least not that she can remember. After she regains her wits, she's looking across the land when she becomes frightened. The grass begins to lay down flat. Bushes and trees start to bend to their extremes. Then it hits. Wind with a huge force almost blows her off of the wall. It would have if she wouldn't have been holding onto the wall.

"Look at that!" Martine yells through the wind.

Isabella looks up. She was frightened, now she's terrified. She can see a white creature flying below the storm. Wings flap, and she knows Cap has arrived. Behind them, a tornado follows. It is humongous! It probably stretches a mile wide, and the destruction she can see is devastating! She climbs off the wall forced to go slow, holding onto anything due to the wind.

She begins running as soon as she hits the ground. The wind half carries her, and she almost flies by the door she's going to. She runs into the building frantically. She stumbles, not prepared for the lack of wind.

She runs back to the room where Captain Gonzales is, and slams the door behind her.

"He's here!" she exclaims, breathing hard.

"Sir Casey?" the captain asks, "Not that I'm not happy to hear it, but there is no way he's got the news yet."

"Well, it's him," she says, "and if the storm is any indication of his mood, I'd say he is *pissed*!"

Breanna bursts into the room, knocking Isabella to her knees and breaking the door. She's followed by a group of her vampires. "Take Diamondback," she tells them, "He's more of a threat to us."

"No," Diamondback says calmly.

"You have no choice," Breanna tells him. The vampires pick him up and begin taking him out of the room.

Diamondback speaks over his shoulder, "Stay with her. She'll need you more than I will." Then he's out of the room and out of sight.

Breanna remains in the room with one other vampire.

"Kill her," she tells the vampire, "Her loyalty is in question." She then leaves the room, talking to herself. "How else could he have known to come so quickly, and during the hours of daylight?" Her voice fades off as she walks away from the room. The vampire left in the room begins salivating with bloodlust.

Captain Gonzales draws his sword, prepared to fight. Isabella stops him. "No, untie them," she orders. The captain lowers his sword, but doesn't sheath it. He backs up to the two restrained men, and releases them, never taking his eyes off the vampire.

The vampire walks towards her slowly. Isabella stands her ground, accepting her fate. The vampire is almost drooling at the thought of such easy prey. The sound of rattles suddenly fills the air. The vampire looks down to see the two snakes on both sides of the woman. It pauses for a moment, and then continues moving forward. Both snakes strike, the rattlesnake pulling back for another strike, the black mamba holding on to its leg. The vampire shrieks with surprise, then pulls the snake off. A chunk of its flesh remains in the mamba's mouth as it throws the snake to the ground.

It begins to float in the air, preparing for an air attack. It falls to the ground suddenly, landing on its stomach. Confused, it tries to float again, but is unsuccessful. The moment of confusion is just enough though. Captain Gonzales rushes the vampire, thrusting his sword into the creature's heart. The vampire falls to the ground dead.

"Should we prepare a defense against Sir Casey?" the captain asks her, wiping his blade clean.

"For god sakes no!" Isabella says, suddenly feeling weak with fear, "I think Breanna wanting to have me killed releases us from our servitude. Have the men stand down, and prepare to fight with Cap."

"Yes Ma'am!" he says, saluting her with a new admiration. He leaves the room in a hurry.

She turns to Adolf and Logan, "Why would Diamondback tell you to stay with me?" she asks them.

"He didn't," Adolf answers.

Logan chuckles, "He told them." He points to the two snakes at her feet.

"Oh," she says looking down, "Thank you." She raises her head back to the two men, "I'm out of my area now. What do we do next?" Adolf and Logan look at each other, and smile menacingly.

Chapter 16

Luke and Martine stand watching the storm upon the ramparts of the wall. The storm has stopped moving for the moment, but the wind persists. Sunlight shines in front of the clouds, illuminating a small part of the landscape. Within the storm though, devastation and turmoil continue to pound the horizon. On the hill, just standing under the storm, a winged horse and one man stand alone. They aren't moving, just looking down at the town. He is too far away to see features.

"Who is that?" Luke asks above the wind.

"I'm not sure," Martine answers him.

Salma climbs up to them, her small body holding on for dear life. "Breanna sends orders. You are to make sure Luke gets out of town, immediately."

"What for?" Luke asks.

"It is only one man," Martine says.

"Because of who it is," Salma answers them. A look of understanding crosses Martine's face.

"And who is it?" Luke asks, anxiously.

"It is Cap," the imp replies.

A look of hatred crosses Luke's face, his eyes showing a hunger for blood. "Kill him!" he yells.

"We can't," Salma opposes, "Remember what Cronus said. That's why you must leave."

Luke's face gets harder with hatred, "Kill him! He's only one man! Every time you all plan our next move, it is always 'What if Cap' this or 'What if Cap' that! Here's an idea. Kill him and you don't have to worry about it! Quit wasting time, and just kill him, here and now! If you won't than I will!"

"But-" Salma tries to complain, but is interrupted by Martine.

"Do it," the werecat orders, "What Luke says makes sense. Send out the zombies. Let's get rid of this problem once and for all."

"I should consult Breanna about this first," Salma says.

"Listen!" Martine yells, picking the imp up, "Breanna can't do anything until it gets dark. That means I'm in charge! Send the zombies!"

"Alright! Alright!" Salma cries out. Martine puts her down, and the imp leaves.

Martine looks back across the field. Cap is still standing in one place. "God, I hope this works," she says, "If it doesn't, both Breanna and Cronus will have our hides."

"I'm not worried," Luke says, "Even if he manages to make it through, I'll finish the job." He looks across to Cap, points to him, and yells, "Let's see what you got!"

On top of the hill, Cap looks down upon the town. He's searching for any sign of where his friends would be kept captive. He watches as the zombies move out of the gate and form a line in front of the wall. He decides to ignore them for the moment. Besides the forces mobilizing, everything appears normal. Everything except...There! One building in the center of town has more guards than any of the rest.

The wind picks up as his anger renews. The thoughts of his friends being tortured replaying in his head. Behind him, the lightning picks up its pace, and the thunder grows even louder. A funnel cloud begins to form above. Hail and rain start to fall all around him. He doesn't notice any of it. His vision is fixated on his mission. Rescue his friends, no matter what it takes. Saving them is all that matters.

Below the hill, in front of the town, the zombies line up in ranks. They are having difficulty in the ferocious wind. Eventually, they get organized and face forward towards Cap. He waits impatiently, wanting to rush in, but not wanting to place his friends in harm's way. He tries to calm his mind. He's alone, and the only way to make this work is to think it out. He looks at the building again. It is almost surrounded by guards now. From what he can see, they all look human. Then he notices the two in front of the door. They get smaller, and then stretch out on all fours. He can't see what they are, but he has a good idea. Werecats.

The movement of zombies brings his attention back to the front of town. They aren't waiting for him to make the first move. So be it. The first rank of zombies begins moving forward. He counts twenty in the line. 'Well,' he thinks, 'I didn't think it would be easy.' From the direction of the town he hears a wolf's howl through the wind. With a renewed vigor, he begins walking forward, Adflictus held tightly and ready to strike. The clouds above begin to move also, blocking the suns light and covering the land in darkness. Only the lightning strikes provide light to see by.

As the zombies reach what could be the halfway point, lightning strikes behind them. Half of them fall to the ground with the concussion of thunder. The other half stop, blinded by the light reflected off of Cap's helmet. Cap rushes in, seizing the opportunity of their confusion. He runs into them, smashing Adfictus' mace into the head of the closest zombie. He spins around, letting his hands slide up to the mace, and swings the spike into another zombie's head. The zombies surround him as their confusion fades away. "Come on!" Cap yells as the tornado touches the ground behind him, covering them in swirling dirt, dust, and debris.

Martine and Luke watch as the lightning gives the fight a strobe light effect. They lose sight as the dirt and dust obliterate any visual that they have. After several minutes, Martine begins to get worried. 'Twenty zombies should have been enough. What is taking so long?' she thinks. It takes several more minutes, but she finds it out. It upsets and frightens her at the same time.

Cap is kneeling on the ground, his head down. All around him are bodies lying still, unmoving. The feathers on top of his helmet move in the wind, the only thing moving in the area. Martine watches with hope. A hope that he is wounded or dead in that position. Cap lifts his head up quickly, shattering her hopes. He stands up, and begins to run towards the town.

With fear in her voice, she yells at the imps behind her, "Two ranks! Send two ranks! Quickly!"

Two ranks of twenty zombies run out on to the field. Cap doesn't slow down a bit. He barrels into them, knocking many of them down. He's clearly close enough now. She can see him move. It fills her with fear to see him swinging with power and speed. The forty zombies have managed to stop his progress, but are having no luck at subduing him. As they close in around him, he fights harder. Bodies are thrown and tossed aside. He's fighting with no concern for himself, and it is giving him the advantage. As she tries to keep track of numbers, she's shocked to see the forty zombies have dropped to half.

"Send in the rest!" she yells at the imps, her voice a full octave higher with fear.

The smell of sweat fills the air as the imps force all of their energy and magic into the fight. She can see the pain in their faces as each zombie is felled. She turns her attention back to the fight, but the hundreds of zombies added to the fight are starting to force him back. She smiles with delight. "It shouldn't be long now," she says, not realizing that Luke isn't beside her.

Cap finds himself fighting for his life. The amount of zombies in the brief light of the lightning seems to be too much. They are backing him up, even though he's holding them back from surrounding him. One zombie tries to sneak behind him, and Cap swings the mace into its temple immediately, throwing his shield up to block a blow directly after. His breath is coming in gasps, and he can feel his muscles getting weary. Lightning flashes all around, allowing him a brief glance of everything. Doubt enters his head, and he disregards it immediately. Fighting harder, he concentrates on his objective.

One by one, the zombies fall, but there is always another to take the place of the previous one. A familiar feeling begins to form within him. He tries to ignore it, not wanting it to take over. The more he ignores it, the stronger it becomes. He continues to fight on, more defending than attacking as his energy drains. With most of his energy gone, he doesn't notice that the zombies have encircled him. Two grab him from behind, immobilizing his attacks. With Adflictus now useless, and his shield to his side, he is defenseless against the dead army. They begin to swarm in on him. The feeling within begins to scream, just begging to burst out. Feeling helpless, and with no other option, he releases it.

His vision brightens the dark world around him with a red tint over everything. Pain and weariness fades from his body as the feeling takes control. Two zombies with daggers rush to stab him. The feeling enters his head at the same moment, and Cap reacts immediately. He bends over quickly, throwing the zombies holding him forward and tripping the two rushing him. Wasting no time, he begins attacking with blows that send zombies flying through the air.

Upon the ramparts of the town wall, Martine watches in horror. 'He was almost killed!' she thinks to herself, 'How could he have gotten out of it?' The speed and power that Cap is displaying terrifies her. It just doesn't seem possible. What's worse, he's not trying to break through the zombies, but is annihilating them! Afraid that he might make it to the walls, she calls for a few of her werecats.

"Get oil," she tells them, "A lot of it. Spread it in front of the gate.

If he makes it this far, we'll block him with a wall of fire!" Her companions hurry away to fulfill her orders.

She watches Cap while she waits. The speed and power he's using can only be compared to either were-beings or vampires. Only, how could he have gotten that kind of ability? It doesn't seem to make sense. Her mouth drops open as she sees him spin around and swing his weapon into a zombie. The thing is hit so hard it flies back, hitting the town wall and falling motionless. Her werecats arrive with lamp oil, and begin to pour it on the ground outside the gate. They reenter the town, taking Martine a lit lamp.

On the field, Cap fights tirelessly. The numbers of the zombies are dwindling very quickly. As less and less remain, the faster and harder he fights. For the moment, all he can think about is destruction. What scares him the most is that he enjoys it. The zombies attempt to back off, an attempt at changing tactics. Cap doesn't let them, diving into them. He's out to destroy them. He's not about to let them retreat.

Time has passed quickly, yet the darkness still remains from the storm. Whether it is night or day, no one can tell. Cap doesn't think on it, but continues to slaughter his foes. He knocks the last one down to the ground, smashing its head into the mud with his boot. He faces the town, taking deep breaths. He walks forward steadily, stepping on and over bodies.

He looks up as he reaches the city walls. He can see the woman standing up there. "Release my friends!" he yells to her, "Now!"

"No!" she yells back at him. She throws the lamp at his feet, and fire consumes the area. Cap within it.

At first, he stands still, shocked. He comes out of his trance, finding it hard to breathe, and searches for an exit, but the fire seems to stretch out in all directions. He drops to his knees, unable to breathe and feeling the scoring pain. From his chest, he feels a warmth not from the fire. He looks down to see a glow coming from the pebble on his chest that the Ifrit gave him. A sudden wind crosses his face, and the fire around him quickly flows into the tiny pebble. Martine looks down at him in complete shock. She doesn't notice Breanna standing next to her.

Breanna yells through the wind to Cap, "Can we negotiate?"

"No!" he yells back, "It's my friends or nothing!"

"What do we get in return?" she asks him.

"Nothing!"

"No deal," she responds to him. She turns to Martine, "Kill him already! Quit playing with him. Where are the zombies?" Martine points to the ground behind Cap. Breanna stares in shock at the devastation. She turns to see all the imps passed out from exhaustion. She's brought back to the sound of pounding. She looks over the wall to see Cap swinging his weapon against the locked gate. With each powerful connection, the gate shakes closer to breaking open.

The sound of splashing water from the river stops Cap. The ground shakes and he can see the Leviathan as lightning strikes beside it. Cap backs away from the gate, allowing him more room to maneuver. The Leviathan strikes at him, and Cap jumps out of the way. He swings his weapon at the creatures head, and it lands with a solid thud. The blow doesn't faze the beast. Cautious and confused, he backs up some more. He looks up at the wall to see Luke laughing. He looks different to Cap. Darker hair, and he looks like he has gained muscle mass.

"This is almost as much fun as killing you myself," Luke calls out to him, "Although, this is more entertaining to watch."

Cap doesn't get a chance to respond. The Leviathan strikes again, and he barely evades its sharp teeth. From within his head a voice speaks to him. 'Use it,' it says.

'What?' Cap thinks, dodging another strike.

'The fire,' it says, 'use the fire.'

"How?" he asks the voice in his head. The Leviathan strikes and Cap can't evade. It clamps down upon his shield, its teeth just barely grazing his skin. It picks him up, shaking him violently, and throws him to the ground. He lands hard, the breath knocked out of him.

'Think of a creature and project it out,' the voice tells him.

Cap rolls out of the way as the beast tries to step on him. He tries to think of the largest and meanest creature that he knows of. He jumps out of the way of another strike, then attempts to project it out. Fire flows out of the pebble, backing the Leviathan towards the river. The fire swirls around, spiraling to an amazing height. It then begins to form quickly into a large animal. Cap stands astonished, not quite believing what he is seeing.

Standing in front of him is a gigantic tyrannosaurus rex! It looks to be fifteen feet tall at the hips, and over forty feet from head to tail. Its hind legs are massive, and its teeth have to be at least six inches long in its U-shaped mouth. Its body stays parallel to the ground, making it seem shorter than the Leviathan. With its large teeth, predator fierceness, and body of fire, what it lacks in size it makes up for in lethality. The fire dinosaur roars its battle cry, drowning out the sound of thunder. Cap has to run out of the way as the giant beasts collide.

Not waiting to see who will be the victor, he runs back to the gate and begins beating on it again. He can feel the door give a little with each strike. The feeling of heat forces him to turn around. The Leviathan has backed up the dinosaur almost to the city walls. The fire beast lands a horrific bite, roars another battle cry and begins attacking with new ferocity. Cap turns his attention back to the gate as the two creatures move away.

He's about to strike at the gate again, when he hears a voice through the wind. "Open the gates!" a female's voice orders. Directly afterwards he hears a gunshot, and a wolf's howl. With a new hope of seeing his friends, he swings Adflictus as hard as he can at the gate. The weapon lands with tremendous force, breaking the gate. He kicks what is left open, and runs through. What he sees angers him.

Breanna has her hand over Isabella's throat, lifting her into the air and chocking the life out of her. Adolf is in his wolf form, dodging and fighting numerous werecats. Logan has his knife out, fending off both vampires and werecats.

"Breanna!" Cap yells out, rushing her. He tackles her below the knees before she can react. She drops Isabella as she falls, rising immediately. Cap is standing over Isabella's unconscious body as Adolf and Logan finish defending themselves and join him. Behind them, Captain Gonzales and the soldiers of El Dorado run to assist.

Breanna calls out to her army, and they fall in behind her. Martine and Luke also join her, with all the werecats. It is a large number of enemies compared to the forces with Cap. Breanna smiles, happy to have another opportunity to match wits of commanders with Cap.

"You are brave, and very stupid," she says to Cap.

"So everyone continues to remind me," Cap replies to her.

"You are outnumbered. Surrender, and I might spare your lives."

Cap looks down at Isabella. He sees the two snakes that accompany Diamondback settle and coil on the sides of her. "Where is he?" he asks, "Where is Diamondback?"

"Somewhere you cannot get to him," she answers.

"Give up my friend," he orders, "If you harm him in any way, so help me God-"

"Your God doesn't reside here!" she interrupts him, "You want him, you'll have to win the fight, or surrender. Look at what you have. I suggest you surrender."

Luke can't wait any longer. "Come here!" he yells with anger. He runs towards Cap, only to be stopped by Breanna.

"Enough! You fool!" she yells at him, "We wouldn't be here if not for you! Martine, get him out of my sight!" Martine says a few words quietly to Luke. His face turns red with anger, and then he turns and walks away.

Breanna speaks very sternly to Cap, "Surrender. Surrender or die."

Cap remains angered, "Not a chance in hell. You'll have to kill me."

"If that is what you want," she raises her hands, and she and her vampires begin to float in the air.

Cap isn't in the mood for her intimidation, nor does he want to wait for her to attack. He grabs the knife out of Logan's hand, and throws it at the vampire. The wind shifts the direction of the knife, and it lands in the heart of the vampire beside her. The vampire falls dead, and Breanna remains where she is, shocked.

Martine moves fast, rushing Cap, trying to catch him off guard. Cap blocks her attack, and throws her to the side. Vampires and werecats attack as one. The battle gets hot and heavy as humans, vampires, and werecats are thrown and perish. Cries of pain and death seem louder than the thunder as the fight goes on. Though Breanna's forces outnumber the humans', Cap's forces stand their ground. Both vampires and werecats attack Cap with each opportunity, but he attacks back with total disregard to himself.

Bodies begin to pile around the unconscious imps and Isabella. Neither side seems to have an advantage, or gain any ground on the other. It is truly a stalemate. Each being seems to be fighting for their own survival, seemingly unaware of any other reason to fight. The fighting is fast and fierce. There is no time to shout orders, for either Cap or Breanna.

All wait for anything from their leaders to win the battle.

Suddenly, the ground begins to shake. The fighting stops and the two sides separate. Cap and Breanna only stand a few yards apart, staring at each other with anger in their eyes. An odd light appears overhead, blue and pink in color. The storm continues to rage. The wall crashes in all of a sudden, the Leviathan and the T-rex both lying on the ground. The two animals pick themselves up, and get behind their chosen sides. Through the broken wall, upon the hill, Heracles and Cuchulain's armies cover the horizon. The strange light is coming from the two goddesses. Cap can see his men are mixed with King Arthur's knights.

Cap smiles triumphantly. "This time," he says to Breanna, "I'm not surrendering the city, and we are not giving up. Surrender. YOU can't win."

Breanna looks at the hill, suddenly ashamed of being defeated again. "I will not surrender," she says to Cap. Fire shows in Cap's eyes, and he smiles as battle cries come from the armies upon the hill. "There is another option," she tells Cap, "We will finish this another day."

Cap, seeing the opportunity of ending the war slipping away, charges at her. She blocks his attack, and throws him to the side. He gets up quickly, ready to fight. Breanna and the vampires are already gone though. He looks around and sees the werecats exiting the west gate of town. He can hear the Leviathan retreating to the river. As he calms down, the realization of victory begins to set in. The thunderstorm begins to disperse, allowing the afternoon sun to shine upon the town.

The armies enter the town to the sounds of cheering from Captain Gonzalez's forces and the townspeople, now brave enough to come out of their homes. Heracles and Cuchulain walk towards Cap wide eyed. They can't hide their surprise of the devastation around their feet. Athena and Aphrodite walk into the town with tears in their eyes. All the lives lost are just too much to hold back their emotions. Heracles and Cuchulain walk up to Cap as the tyrannosaurus transforms back into fire, and returns to the pebble on Cap's chest.

"Wow," Cuchulain says, "If you would have waited just a little longer, there might have been some left for us."

"There was no time," Cap says with disappointment in his voice, "and I was still too late."

"It looks like you were just in time," reassures Heracles.

Cap looks around. "Too many lives lost," he says, "and one not recovered." He walks away from them. They let him go knowing that anything they could say won't help. They watch as Cap stops to the sound of moaning. The imp Salma gets up very slowly. "Grab her," Cap orders. Two men obey, grabbing the arms of the small creature.

Cap continues walking on. He stops when he reaches Isabella. He kneels down beside her. She is still unconscious, and is breathing abnormally. He picks her up off the ground and looks around. He sees an older looking man. Cap recognizes him as one of the elders.

"She needs a room," Cap says walking up to him.

The old man smiles at her limp body. "No," he says cheerfully, "I won't allow it. Do you know what she did?"

Cap's face gets hard with anger, "Does it look like I care? A room, now, or you'll join the rest of the bodies lying here on the ground!"

The elder is about to deny him again, but the look of death in Cap's eyes changes his mind. He lowers his head, afraid to look Cap in the eyes. "This way," he says disappointed.

The old man walks away, and Cap begins to follow. He turns his head and calls behind him, "Bring the lead imp to me, and lock up the others." He continues following the old man, talking to himself, "There may be some use for them. There may just be…"

Chapter 17

Isabella wakes in a cold sweat. She can still feel Breanna's hand around her throat. It feels like a dream, and Breanna's angry face haunts every moment. Her breath begins to slow as she realizes she is no longer in danger. The dawn sun is beginning to brighten the golden room. She looks out the window, very confused.

"What happened?" she asks herself out loud.

"Sh," Isabella hears to her left.

She almost jumps out of bed with fright. She turns her head to see Salma straightening the sheets on the bed. Her face turns grim. 'We lost,' she thinks. The imp puts a finger up to her mouth to signal silence. She then points across the bed. Isabella turns her head towards the area pointed. She sees Cap asleep in the chair beside the bed. He seems to be sleeping very soundly.

Isabella turns back to the imp. "What happened?" she whispers.

Salma shrugs her shoulders, "He won," she whispers back, "He defeated Breanna, again."

"Am I a prisoner?" Isabella asks.

"No, but I am," the imp answers, pointing to a chain around one of her ankles.

"How?"

Salma points to Cap again, "We used all of our strength with the entire zombie army. He destroyed them all as we passed out from the exertion. I don't know what happened between that and when I woke up."

"He took on all the zombies!?"

"Yeah, and with ability I've never seen before!"

Isabella suddenly gets self-conscious. Her hand goes to her chest where her medallion should be. Her eyes get wide when she doesn't feel it.

She looks around the room frantically, but it is nowhere to be seen. She looks at Cap, then back to Salma. "Does he know?" she asks.

"Yes," Salma answers, "I was forced to tell him."

"Oh," Isabella says, disappointed.

"He didn't take it bad," Salma says, trying to cheer her up, "He said a lot of great rulers gained power through questionable means. He listed several names, but I only recognized Octavias Caesar and Alexander the Great."

"Really? Wow!" she exclaims, trying to be quiet. "So, did I lose it?" she asks, patting her chest.

"No, it is on the table beside you," Salma tells her, "Not that the elders didn't try. They convinced a large part of the town to take the position from you. Cap wouldn't allow it. The elders persisted till Captain Gonzales stood beside Cap. Then the heroes walked up. That ended the small rebellion, without a single blow! Cap then had the two goddesses take over your duties until you recover."

"Two goddesses? It all sounds like a fairy tale," Isabella says, "It just doesn't seem real."

"It is very real," Cap says suddenly, startling both of them, "I'm glad to see you awake. And feeling better, I hope."

"Yes," she says, lowering her head, suddenly embarrassed, "Thank you."

"Don't mention it. Salma will assist you with anything you need. I'll go get you some breakfast." He gets out of the chair, stretching real quickly, and leaves the room.

As soon as Isabella is sure that he's gone, she asks Salma another question, "What is it about him? He has a commanding air about him, but he is not commanding. It is very confusing."

Salma smiles at her, "That is the sign of a good leader. His commands are obeyed, but he doesn't demand it, usually. The people follow him because they believe in him."

"I always thought that being a leader was more than that," Isabella says.

"So did I," Salma agrees, "so did I." She changes her tone, "We need to get you dressed before he gets back. Come, my lady."

Isabella throws the covers off of herself. She stands up as Salma hands her an elegant long sleeved emerald green dress. It is trimmed with gold lace around the neck and cuffs of the sleeves. Unlike her other dress, she can see that it is very form fitting, showing every curve of her body. She looks at herself in a full length mirror on the door. "Wow!" she says with surprise, "It is gorgeous!"

"Cap picked it out for you," Salma tells her, "I'm sure he'll be pleased that you like it."

Isabella blushes, "You sound like you admire him yourself."

"It is hard not to," she responds, "He is caring and compassionate. When the topic came up of what to do with us prisoners, he was most adamant about not torturing us. Even though everyone else was for it. How did he put it? 'There is nothing good that could come of torture. Only pain and misery.' he said"

"You were there?"

"Yes. Cap wouldn't explain why. Just that he said I needed to be there."

Isabella gets a confused look on her face, "I wonder what he's planning."

"I wish I could tell you. We are kept locked up in a building, or chained. He made me take care of you, and ordered the rest of my imps to use our magic to heal all of the injured soldiers. Besides that, you wouldn't be able to tell we are prisoners. He makes sure we are treated with respect and dignity. It is very unusual. We would never have treated him in the same manner. He is using our magic, but he's not using us for battle reasons. I also wish I knew what he was up to."

Her thoughts are interrupted by a knock on the door and Cap's voice, "Is it safe to come in?"

"Yes," Isabella answers. The door opens and Cap walks in with a tray covered by a large cloth napkin. He sets it on the table under the window, and pulls it out in front of the bed. He steps outside, grabs two chairs, then brings them in and sets them opposite of each other at the table.

"Please, join me ladies," he says, holding a chair for Isabella. Soon as she's seated, he makes sure that Salma is seated. "Now, for your dining pleasure," he says rubbing his hands together, "I would like to offer you what my family affectionately calls The Goose Pit Breakfast." He lifts the napkin from the tray to reveal three plates, "Scrambled eggs mixed with chopped pieces of ham, pepper, onions, and fried potatoes." He sets a plate in front of each of them, and hands them a fork. He sits on the bed between them, grabbing a plate for himself. "Dig in," he tells them. He waits until they are both eating, then begins eating himself.

"This is good," Isabella says. Salma nods her head in agreement.

"Thank you," Cap says, "I haven't had the chance to cook for a while, so I took this opportunity when I got it." They all continue eating. Cap finishes, and waits until his companions are also done.

"There is something I wanted to discuss, also," he says.

Salma's face gets a concerned shade across it, "And that would be?"

"A few things, actually," he tells her, "First, I need to know if you and the imps have been treated fairly."

"Very much so," she replies, "I would like to thank you for that. It was, and still is, very unexpected."

"Your welcome. Now, I would also like to run an idea by you. I hope it doesn't offend you. How would you feel about joining us?"

"What?" she says, very surprised, "This must be a joke. Surely, you must be joking."

"It is no joke," Cap says, "and I am very sure of it."

"I'm not so sure that is such a good idea," Salma says.

"Oh," Cap says, sounding sarcastically surprised, "Why is that?"

"We aren't exactly accepted by any of the humans. Most frown on our practice of using zombies for battle," she tells him.

"That can be easily changed," he contradicts.

"Really?" she asks, "You would want to use our zombies in your army?"

"Good god no!" he says quickly, "Let the dead rest in peace."

"Then what would you want us for?" she asks, very confused.

He smiles confidently at her, "For medicinal purposes."

"Huh?" she asks confused.

"Your magic can bring the dead back to life. I can understand how that would gain a reputation of being something evil. From my studies, as I understood it, imps are misunderstood creatures. Your magic can also be used to heal. You all have proven that already." He wait's a moment for the information to sink in. "I'm offering sanctuary and friendship. All I ask for in return is for the imps to use their magic to heal the sick and injured when the time comes."

"Are you sure that's all you want in return?" Salma asks,

"Well," he says with a smile, "A little insight into how the enemy does things from time to time wouldn't hurt."

"I see," she says, contemplating the idea.

"Well," Cap says, "What do you think?"

"It does sound very tempting," she replies.

"But?" he asks.

"I would be a traitor, and I would make traitors of my imps also. I'm not sure I would want that for us," she answers.

"Salma," Isabella says, "Breanna ordered me killed because she *thought* I might have told Cap about the siege. I didn't. You've even said that the way he's treated you was very kind. You know her better than I do, but I doubt she'll believe you were treated fairly. I think that she would consider you a traitor because of the kindness he has shown you, and all the imps. You should really take that into consideration."

Salma gets a tormented look on her face. She closes her eyes, and thinks of both consequences of choosing either side. "I still don't know," she says quietly.

"What do you think could happen?" Cap asks.

"If we join you?" Salma asks, raising her eyebrows, "We will be branded as traitors. Breanna and Cronus will both be after our heads. We will be targeted as much, if not more than you."

"And if you don't?" he asks.

"We remain prisoners, locked and chained. We will be at the mercy of you and everyone else. You have been kind to us, so far. How long would it last if we chose not to join you, I wonder?" she looks up at him, sadness and worry in her eyes.

Cap looks at her, understanding the worry. He is determined to recruit her to join him, but he doesn't want to force her. There is no way of telling what the wrath of an imp could do, nor does he want to find out. He must tread very carefully. He doesn't want to anger her. "Why do you raise the dead?" he asks suddenly.

Salma looks at him oddly, as if he should already know. "For our protection," she answers, "Our bodies aren't designed well to defend well against others, and magic can only go so far."

"What does it feel like?" he asks, "I mean, does it do anything to you, emotion wise?"

She closes her eyes, and thinks back. "It can be very painful," she says, "All of their pain, worry, and sorrow they felt when they died we feel when they are raised. It takes a lot of energy, so there can be physical pain also."

Cap nods his head, not understanding, but knowing pain. He pulls out a key, gets off the bed and releases her from her chains. "I'm not saying things will be easy. I can't offer relief from the pain. If you were to join us though, you wouldn't have to go through it again. You would be protected. You won't be forced into such drastic measures again. It may not sound like much. Yet, how much would it take for peace of mind?"

The chain lies still on the floor as Salma stares at it with bewilderment. What he says is right. Peace of mind shouldn't take much. No more torment, no more pain, it all sounds extremely tempting. Having the protection from someone other than dead slaves also attracts her to the idea. She looks at Cap and Isabella. Even as prisoners, they are treating her as an equal. Something she never felt with Breanna or Martine.

"How can I be sure about all this?" she asks them.

Isabella remains silent, unsure herself. Cap shrugs his shoulders, "I can give you my word. That may not mean anything, but it is a start. Truth is, it will take some time. It will take time for the people to get used to the idea. If you help, and be honest in what you do, it will take much less time. By the look in your eyes, it shouldn't take too long."

"How can you sound so sure?" Salma asks.

"Because I am," he replies, "If I didn't believe in it myself, no one ever will. I do believe, and others will too, eventually."

She looks down at the chain again. That is an enormous risk, allowing an enemy to roam free. It is a large sign of trust. She gets a feeling that she can't explain from it. Something she has never felt before. She tries to vision her future, and she doesn't see herself hiding in the dreary Bergsrå Mountains anymore, but on the sunny wide open plains of Immortalis. Surrounded by friends, she sees something of herself. True happiness, with a true smile and a cheery attitude.

"It all sounds good," she says, "We will join you. But only on one condition."

"What's that?" Cap asks.

"If we aren't treated well, or are discriminated against, we will be free to leave. Without any consequences," she tells him.

Cap smiles, happy that she chose to join them. "You have my word. I won't hold you with us against your will." He begins to pick the dishes up, then stops, "Before I leave, there is one thing. There is a meeting in a few minutes, if I'm not late already. I'd like both of you to go. If you are feeling up to it, of course."

Isabella looks up at him, "I think I'm ready."

"I will," Salma says.

"Good!" Cap says smiling, "I will see you both there. It is at the same building that Isabella will govern from." He picks up the tray, and leaves the room.

Isabella and Salma both get up from their chairs, and leave the small room. As they walk out of the building and on to the street, Isabella speaks to Salma, "I'm glad you have decided to join us."

"I'm not joining all of you," Salma states, "I'm joining him. It might sound bad, but he seems to believe everything he says, and I respect that. There is something about him that I trust, also. I've never felt that around any other humans. Even you."

Isabella doesn't respond, feeling a little disappointed. They walk through the street to the largest building in town. Knights' horses, and numerous soldiers around it make it a tell-tale sign that this is where the meeting is taking place. The two walk in, while people standing by and stare in wonder at the free walking imp. She pays them no mind, walking with Isabella into a very well lit room with lots of windows. The amount of light in the room gives it an optimistic feeling. Much different than the windowless room Breanna used. At least from Salma's perspective.

The room is filled with people, making its size seem irrelevant. There is a square table in the middle without any chairs. The table is much too small for everyone in the room, making Salma wonder what it is used for. The talking in the room slowly ceases as people begin to realize the small imp's presence. The idea of showing at this meeting doesn't seem like a good idea anymore to Salma.

The room gets silent as death. One man gets the courage to speak. "What's that doing here?" he asks meanly.

"She's been released," Isabella says with a commanding air, "She has also been invited."

"By who?" he asks.

"By me," Cap's voice rings through the quiet room. He walks in carrying a rolled up paper in his arms, "Any questions?" He waits for a few moments, but no one speaks, "Alright then. I need these people. Logan, Adolf, Cuchulain, Athena, Isabella, Sir Palomedes, and Salma. I need Heracles and Aphrodite to remain outside the room. Everyone else, if you would, please exit the building." Grumbling is heard throughout the room, and a few leave right away. Others wait, hoping that Cap will change his mind. "Now, please," he says with aggravation, "We don't have time to waste." Reluctantly, everyone but those asked for, leave the room.

When they have the room to themselves, Adolf asks, "What is going on?"

"Rescue mission," Cap answers bluntly.

"What?" Logan asks, surprised.

"I want to set up a rescue mission for Diamondback," Cap says.

Cuchulain looks at Cap, "I understand that you want to save your friend, but it is pointless. There is no way of knowing where he could be."

"That's not exactly true," Cap tells him, "We have something that they don't."

"And what would that be?" Athena asks.

"Insight and knowledge," he answers her, pointing to Isabella and Salma. He unrolls the paper on the table. "Come around. This should give you a hint."

They gather around the table. On the table lies a map of Immortalis. Everyone looks at each other with confusion. This hint isn't much, and yet no one is willing to ask questions. They stand there silently, waiting for Cap to explain.

"Now," he begins, "Where would they likely hold their prisoner?" he asks all of them, but looking at Salma.

Salma looks around at everyone, shy and unsure of what they are thinking. None seem to be looking at her though. They are looking at the map. Salma points a finger to the Bergsrå Mountains. "Around here," she says, "That is where Cronus keeps his military meetings at. That would be the most likely place."

"How could we get there without being seen?" Cap asks, "It is out of the way of the Hamingja Road."

"We flew," she says, "We didn't use the roads."

"What about the zombies?" Adolf asks, "They can't fly."

"They just followed," she answers, "I have no idea how they made it."

"Well," Cap says, "Any ideas?"

"You could send a small group out to find a way," Athena suggests.

"Reconnaissance? That could work," Cap says, thinking, "We would need to sneak by their entire force then."

"How will we be able to accomplish that?" Isabella asks.

Cap is silent for a moment, lost in thought. He smiles mischievously all of a sudden. "Logan, Adolf? Think you would be able to find a way there?"

The two men look over the map. Their eyes move along it, searching for hidden trails. The map is crude, and only shows the Hamingja Road vividly. No side roads or trails are visible. They look at each other, thinking similar thoughts.

"It is possible," Logan says.

"Only, getting around Avalon might be a bit of a problem," Adolf adds.

"Would a diversion help?" Cap asks.

"How would you do that?" Logan asks.

"By feigning a blow," Cap responds, smiling, "Cuchulain, ask Heracles to come in, please." Cuchulain leaves the table and pokes his head out of the room. He turns around, and walks back to the group. Heracles comes into the room, closes the door behind him, and walks to the table. "Heracles," Cap says, "Think you can have your men ready for a raid on Avalon?"

"Yes," Heracles answers, "It wouldn't take too much."

"Great!" Cap exclaims, "Here's what I have in mind. I want you and your army to make a show of force against Avalon. I don't want you to attack it, but get them scrambling. That should be enough to give their lookouts tunnel vision. While that is going on, Adolf, Logan, Cuchulain, and I should be able to get by the town undetected. Before night falls, pull back. Don't get your men killed over this.

"From there, we'll go into the mountains. Once we find a suitable place to hole up, Adolf and Logan can scout a way to Cronus' hiding place. You two will be harder to detect, so I'm hoping you won't mind. If Diamondback is there, the four of us will go in together. If he is injured, Cuchulain, you will have to carry him back. The three of us will cover you. But if things get bad, we will need your speed to get Diamondback out of there, and out of danger.

"I'm planning to sneak by Avalon during the day, so we'll have to return before darkness falls, if possible. I can only hope to be as stealthy as you three. So if we're noticed, you get back to El Dorado as fast as you possibly can. Leave me behind. Once everyone is safe and sound, we can plan what we'll do next. So? What do you think?"

"I think it is too much to gamble on," Sir Palomedes answers, There are too many factors that could go wrong. The slightest mistake and you all will be doomed."

"Breanna will be expecting something like this," Isabella tells them, "She may be over confident, but she's not stupid."

"Will she be with Diamondback?" Cap asks.

"Most likely not," she answers, "Avalon is their staging point. She will be making preparations there."

"That works out perfectly," Cap says, "At least for our little invasion. Getting back might be a different story."

"What will the rest of us be doing?" Sir Palomedes asks.

"Spreading the word," Cap answers, "Make everyone think Heracles *is* going to attack Avalon. Make sure that is all everyone can talk about."

"And when do you plan on doing this?" Heracles asks.

"Immediately," Cap says, "I want to be near Avalon by morning. Have the knights help you prepare. When we are gone, Athena and all of the knights will be in charge of defense. Will that work, governor?"

"I have no complaints," Isabella replies.

"Ok, then. Have Aphrodite move throughout the town," he says off impulse, "If there is another spy in El Dorado, they will likely say something to her. Her beauty is too distracting. Don't let anyone else know about the rescue besides the people in this room. The less that know, the better." He looks around, expecting opposition. Not one of them argues, so he says, "Alright, let's get moving." Everyone leaves the room, except Cap and Isabella.

"Cap? Are you sure this is going to work?" she asks.

"It has to," he says, "There isn't any room for failure."

Chapter 18

"What the hell were you thinking!?" Breanna screams as she throws a table across the dimly lit room. Martine and Luke both duck underneath it, letting it shatter into pieces upon the wall behind them.

"We thought it would benefit the campaign to be rid of Cap," Martine answers her, fear hiding within her voice.

"And what possessed you two to be so bold? Who gave you the power to make such decisions?" Breanna asks angrily, "Not only did you fail your objective, but we've lost the town and the imps as well! Without the imps, the zombies are useless! Only undead creatures walking around confused! IF there are any left! Did that cross your minds? Did *anything* cross your minds?"

"How were we to know that he would be able to fight an entire army of zombies?" Luke asks, "That would have been good information to have beforehand. Where were your spies on that one?"

"You have NO right to question me!" she quips back at him, "He is your brother. YOU should know what he is capable of."

"I was supposed to know?" Luke asks surprised, "You need to use your head. There is no *way* I could have known!"

"This isn't getting us anywhere," Martine interrupts, "What do we do next?"

Cronus' voice rings through the room, "You quit bickering." He isn't in sight, but his presence can be felt. "You can't continue without help, and help is what I'm getting for you. You will be assisted by help that I have been recruiting. You will stay in Avalon until they arrive. Understand?"

"Clearly, sire," Breanna says. The small group remains silent, waiting for Cronus' presence to leave. They only wait for a moment, but the silent waiting feels like it is much longer.

"I have a question," Luke says, breaking the silence, "How did Cap get that fire beast?"

"I wish I knew," Martine says, "A beast like that would come in very handy."

"Quit dwelling on it!" Breanna orders, "Daylight is coming and I need rest. DO NOT do anything without consulting me first. We don't need to make the same mistake twice!" She turns abruptly, and leaves the room.

Martine picks up a piece of broken table and throws it angrily across the room. "What is going on?" she yells, "How? How in the hell was he able to defeat us?" She asks, throwing her head back. Luke doesn't answer her, but stands silent while she continues, "This Cap defeated our entire zombie army single handedly! He conjured a fire creature out of nowhere to fight the Leviathan. He broke through the gate with no help. When he did get in, he had the town's militia behind him! All the while, he distracted us just enough to allow reinforcements to arrive without incident!" she turns to Luke, "He *is* your brother. There must be something you know about him that could help us."

"I don't know," Luke says disappointed, "This is all new to me also. I've never seen him like this. He is someone new, someone dangerous. He is nothing that he was before. I don't know anything that could help."

"I just want to know," Martine says, changing the subject, "How did he do it? That information alone would be helpful."

"You know," Luke says, with an optimistic look, "Knowing how isn't near as important as knowing he can."

"Huh?" she asks, "Explain."

"We know what he can do. We know his capabilities. Our

advantage is that we can figure out a counter to what he can do."

"You sound optimistic about it, but how? How could we possibly counter him?"

"By finding something that can fight his fire creature, for one. Having a defense against this new speed and strength is another. Using his fears against him is another."

"A creature that can fight will be easy enough to find. Creating defenses against him will also, but what are his fears?"

"The last I knew, he was afraid of fire. That no longer seems to be the case. I don't know what his fear is now. I only hope that we can find one before it is too late."

"Then we'll have to find out what it is, and some way to use that against him. The sea is to the south. It is a little out of the way, yet not far from Elysian Fields. If we could lure him and his forces to that area, we may be able to isolate him. That might just be the advantage we've been looking for! Let's run the idea by Breanna. I doubt she'll disagree to it, but you never know." Luke nods his head in agreement.

Sunlight enters the room from a window high on the wall. They both step into the light, bathing in its warmth. The silence seems cleansing, and it allows their heads to think clearly. Thoughts of attacks, and counter attacks enter their minds. The only sound in the room is their breathing. Their thoughts are interrupted by a knock at the door.

"Mistress," a small female werecat enters her head through the doorway, "There is something out her you need to see."

"Now what," Martine says aggravated, "Let's go." They walk out of the building, through the streets, and climb onto the east wall.

On the horizon, just below the rising sun is a large army lined up in battle formation. At first, Martine thinks it is her imagination. She closes her eyes, and shakes the image out of her head. She opens her eyes to see the army is still there. Her mouth drops open in surprise.

"There is no way," she says to herself with shock, "They can't possibly think they can take Avalon back!" She turns to Luke, "Go tell Breanna. She won't be able to help until nightfall, but she may have some ideas. And she won't kill us for not telling her."

"Alright," Luke says, "Is Cap with them?"

"I can't tell," she answers, "They are too far away to tell. I bet that he is up there somewhere though. Now go!" Luke jumps down from the wall, and runs towards the castle.

Martine begins shouting orders to everyone around her, "Defense positions! Immediately! Get everyone ready for battle! We are on our own until nightfall. Move it!"

Werecats begin to scramble all around Avalon. Many searching for werecats not at their posts. Lookouts leave their places and get to their assigned fighting positions, on the ground and upon the wall. Everyone is moving around. To the south, barely in view, a small group of people slip past the town unnoticed.

Chapter 19

The sun is high in the sky, bringing unbearable heat upon the ground. Cap and Cuchulain rest beneath the mountain trees, waiting for Adolf and Logan to return. The two left to scout for a hidden way to Cronus' lair. Where they are at right now, the trees and undergrowth are very thick. This makes it easier to sneak up to the lair without being seen, but almost impossible to be silent.

Cuchulain naps in the shade as Cap rests against a tree. He is tired from traveling all night and into the day, yet his mind won't allow him to rest. Luke's face keeps popping into his thoughts. He was almost unrecognizable in El Dorado. His hair was almost black, and he had gotten much more muscular. He may have even been taller, but Cap isn't sure. What happened to his brother? Even his look of hatred towards him was fiercer than ever before.

He picks up a stick and begins drawing on the ground. It is nothing recognizable, just something to clear his mind while he waits. The sound of rustling leaves brings him and Cuchulain to their feet, ready to fight. Adolf and Logan walk up to them. Cap and Cuchulain remain weary though, unsure if they had been followed.

"We've found it," Logan says, "It is a cave not far from here. There is a game trail we can follow that will get us close without being seen."

"Great!" Cap says, "Let's get going. If we're lucky, we can get past Avalon before it gets dark."

"That will probably be easier said than done," Adolf tells him.

"Why is that?" Cuchulain asks, "It seems simple enough."

"Nothing is simple in Immortalis," Logan says, "It'd be easier if we show you." He and Adolf turn around and head through the forest, Cap and Cuchulain behind them.

The brush is thick, and very difficult to walk through, climbing over bushes and crawling under branches. The Terrain goes on like this for about a hundred yards. They then enter a small clearing with a very small dirt trail on which to follow. The game trail appears to extend through the forest without any hindrances. They are all very careful to make sure nothing is around, or traveling, before they step onto the game trail. The last thing they need is to be discovered by accident.

The four men follow the trail towards the west. Sometimes they get closed in by trees and bushes, but their way is still passable. Logan and Adolf slow down as they get closer to a small break in the bushes. Adolf points through the opening, indicating Cap and Cuchulain should take a look. From their current position, they can see an open path to the cave. Cap's face is frozen in shock. In front of the opening is a red haired giant guarding the entrance!

"What the heck is that?" Cap asks, whispering.

"It is Cacus," Adolf whispers back, "He is a fire breathing giant."

"I half expected to see the hell hound," Cap states.

"That's Hades' pet," Adolf explains, "Before we can get into the cave, we need to get past that thing."

They stare at the opening, thinking of different ways to get by the creature. It sits upon a boulder, holding what looks like a large turkey in its hands. It takes a deep breath, and blows a stream of fire. The smell of cooking meat fills the air. After seconds pass, the giant takes in a breath, revealing a golden brown cooked bird. It eats it ravenously, grease streaming from its chin.

"Ok," Cap says, "This could be a slight problem. Any ideas?"

"Do you still think it is hungry?" Cuchulain asks humorously. The creature burps loudly, and begins looking around eagerly.

"I'd say that is a yes," Logan answers.

Cap stands up straight, "Well, let's give him something to chase then."

"Now what are you thinking?" Adolf asks.

Cap doesn't answer him, just says, "As soon as he is out of the way, get in there. I'll try to catch up later."

"I don't like this" Logan tells him.

"Neither do I," Cap responds, "I'm just winging it. If Diamondback is in there, we can't afford to waste time thinking about it. You three are far stealthier than I am. I have no doubt that I can elude the giant, but there is no way I could get Diamondback out of there undetected." He looks back out towards the Cacus, "Well, I guess now is as good of time as any." He walks toward the cave very casually, not allowing his companions any chance to argue.

"Excuse me," Cap says loudly, attracting the giant's attention, "Something smells like chicken. Is there any left?"

The giant looks at him with shock, and then with hungry eyes. It extends out its right hand and tries to grab Cap. Cap jumps out of the way, and the giants hand misses him by inches. Cap mentally yells at himself for being too complacent. More cautiously, he steps back within reach.

"Hey, dumb dumb," he yells, trying to sound angry, "I came to dinner, not as dinner. Are you too stupid to understand?"

The Cacus' look of hunger changes quickly into anger. It stands up, towering over everything except the trees and the mountain. It raises a fist high above its head.

"Ah, snap!" Cap yells out loud as the giant brings his fist down. Cap rolls to his left, just avoiding being smashed. Angrier, the Cacus raises his leg and attempts to stomp Cap into the ground. Cap dives out of the way, the giant's foot missing by a hair.

"Ok," Cap says, getting up quickly, "Time to go."

Cap takes off running away from the cave. The Cacus yells something that can't be understood, and loud enough to vibrate everything around. It takes off running after Cap, breaking tree branches and shaking the ground. Adolf, Cuchulain, and Logan just watch in disbelief.

"He's out of his mind," Adolf says.

"Yeah," Cuchulain agrees, "but he gave us an opening."

They leave the bushes and move cautiously to the cave. Peering inside, it looks like a normal cave, except for the red light within. They walk in very slowly, keeping their senses tuned for anything. On the far wall, Diamondback is hanging upside down. He appears to be sleeping as they walk up to him. They *hope* he is sleeping.

"Let me down easy," Diamondback says when they get close enough, "I've been hangin' here for a couple days." He opens his eyes and looks at the three men. "I wasn't expecting to be rescued," he says as they cut the rope and let him down gently. "Better help me out of here, at least till the blood gets back into my legs."

They all chuckle silently as Diamondback puts his arms around Adolf's and Cuchulain's necks. They walk slowly out of the cave, both cautious and attempting to let him recover. Their pace quickens when they get into the open. They stop when they're back on the game trail. Diamondback's face is still red with blood, but is starting to clear up.

"Where is Cap?" Diamondback asks, "I know I heard his voice."

"He's off playing hero with the Cacus," Logan answers him.

"Is he stupid?" Diamondback asks incredulously.

"We were wondering the same thing," Logan answers.

Diamondback gives Logan a confused look, "Do we wait and help him?"

"He said he'd catch up," Adolf replies, "We can wait for him back at the clearing. Think you can walk now?"

"Yeah," he answers, "I'll be fine."

They walk slowly down the trail, and then pick up the pace as Diamondback's legs get closer to normal. The air is hot, even with the sun getting closer to hiding behind the mountain. The silence around them keeps them weary. There are no birds singing, or any other sounds besides their own footsteps. They jump off the trail as the sound of breaking branches comes to their ears. Looking behind them, they can see Cap running towards them. They step back onto the trail to greet him. They can see him breathing hard, but it looks like he is smiling.

"Run!" Cap yells at them.

They take off as a thudding sound begins to get closer. Looking behind them, they can see the Cacus gaining ground. Cap stops and turns around. He spreads his arms out, and the Cacus stops. Cap's companions stop and watch as the giant blows out a stream of fire at Cap. Cap stands still as the fire surrounds him. It swirls around him, and then flows into the pebble on his chest.

Cap stands with his arms wide open, smiling. "BOO!" he yells at the giant. The giant gets a surprised look on its face, then turns around and runs away.

Cap turns around and runs towards his friends. "I can't get enough of that," he says to them, laughing.

"It will kill you one of these days," Logan says to him, "Let's get out of here before he comes back." Cap nods his head, and they take off running down the trail.

They reach the clearing of their camp, and stop to rest. The sun is beginning to set behind the mountain, drowning the land in eerie shadows. To stay and rest is what they would all like, but they know they must keep moving. They catch their breaths, and begin moving back towards the east.

They hurry down the mountain, eager to be on the plains before night falls. They know their chances of survival will diminish if they are on the mountain when it gets dark. The creatures that will come out will be deadly, and they don't want to imagine what those will be. The sky begins to turn red, and they run hard to reach the plains.

Stars begin to show their light as Avalon comes into view. They slow to a walk, swinging wide to the south to avoid the town. The armies of Heracles aren't within sight. Cap feels disappointment at this, but he was expecting it. He did give Heracles the order to withdraw before it began to get dark. They try to lower themselves beneath the grass to hide themselves, unaware of the eyes that are upon them.

Chapter 20

Luke had been staring at the eastern horizon all day. The opposing army never made a move. It just sat there, as if it were mocking them. Almost begging them to come attack. Breanna had ordered Martine to wait for them to attack, and that is exactly what they did. Reluctantly and anxious, ready for action all day, but they waited none the less. Something is bothering him though. Something is leaving him uneasy. Something isn't right.

Cap enters his thoughts. His younger brother was more confident than he has ever seen him before. He stood straighter. His eyes shown brighter than any other time he has looked in them. For all of the years they have known each other, they are more different now than ever before. Fitting, actually, since he no longer considers Cap his brother anymore.

He keeps looking back west. A feeling, or maybe a premonition, but something is troubling him in that direction. Darkness reaches Avalon as the sun sets, but it no longer bothers him. He can see in the dark better than he ever before. He knows it is because of what he has become. He is stronger than ever. He can see better and farther than any human. He likes it. In fact, he loves it.

Movement catches his eye to the south, and he stares into the darkness towards it. It is difficult to see at first, but as it gets closer, it becomes clearer. The movement is a small group of people walking low in the tall grass. They are indiscernible, the grass giving them just enough cover. Something reflects in the starlight. Luke recognizes it as the orange feathered crest on Cap's helmet. He almost laughs at the sight. 'He should know better. I taught him better than that,' he thinks to himself.

Knowingly disobeying Breanna's orders, he quietly sneaks out of town. He moves slowly and silently. He stops at the bank of the river, peering into the open area not to get caught. The river is shallow at this point. He is able to wade across it in total silence. He hides himself quickly in the brush on the bank. Evil thoughts enter his mind, and he laughs within at them.

He moves through the grass with amazing stealth. He comes upon the bent grass of the small group. He follows them staying far back, but close enough to see how many there are. Five in all. Cap is the easiest to see. The colors of his clothing shine in the dark with his vision. The red and orange almost shine like the sun with his new vision. 'The fool,' he thinks, 'I know I taught him much better than that.' His pace quickens, a predator stalking his prey.

Luke steps on a twig by mistake. The twig cracks loudly in the silent night. The group stops immediately, frozen in motion. They turn around slowly, tense and ready to fight. Luke recognizes Diamondback, sensing his weakness. His time in captivity was enough. He won't be able to defend himself. The others can though, and he is alone.

"Cap," he says quietly.

"Luke," Cap answers back.

"I only want you," Luke says, "no one else."

"So you can kill me? Why should I let you?"

"This is between you and me. The rest aren't involved. Neither your side or mine."

"That is a worthless argument, and you know it."

Luke shrugs his shoulders, "Then let us call it what it is. Pride. We both know this won't end while both of us are alive. And I won't stop until you are dead."

"Your point?"

"Let's end this."

"Now isn't the time."

"It is the time!" Luke growls, "If you won't fight me now, I'll kill you one by one until you are the only one left! And I'll start with Diamondback."

Cap looks at Diamondback. He is ready to fight, but Cap can tell that he is still too weak. The captivity and traveling just took too much out of him. "Get Diamondback out of here," he says.

"Cap, that's not wise," Cuchulain tells him.

"Luke's right," Cap says, looking at Luke, "This is between him and me. Get out of here and to safety. If I don't make it back, you know why. Now go!"

Reluctantly, Cap's four companions leave. Cap and Luke begin circling each other very slowly. Neither allows the other out of their sight. Neither says a single word. They just size each other up, hoping to find a disadvantage. With only the stars showing this dark night, it appears that Luke has the advantage. Cap's orange and red armor shine brightly in the dim starlight. Luke is difficult to see in the dark, dressed all in black. Slowly he pulls a dagger from his belt.

"Are you ready to die, brother?" Luke asks.

"Ready as I'll ever be," Cap answers.

Luke strikes at Cap, and Cap blocks with his shield. Luke backs off a bit, smiling. He pulls out another dagger, and strikes again. Cap blocks both blows. One with his shield, and the other with Adflictus. Luke's smile fades away. He attacks Cap with fierce hatred. Purposely, he leaves openings for Cap to strike back, but his brother doesn't make a move towards him.

"Fight me!" Luke yells at him.

"No," Cap says.

"You have to!"

"No."

Luke moves in, slicing and stabbing. He uses everything he knows and has learned with the daggers, but Cap is able to block everything. Metal hits metal, and sparks fly. Luke swings at Cap, and Cap ducks underneath, tapping Luke on the back. Infuriated, he strikes harder and faster. Still, he is unable to harm Cap.

Backing up, Luke asks, "Why won't you fight me?"

"You are my brother," Cap answers, "I'm not going to fight you."

"We haven't been brothers since you dishonored me."

"I didn't dishonor you!" Cap yells at him.

"BULL!" Luke yells back.

A large red moon begins to rise in the east, spreading an eerie light upon the land. The light gives Cap a clearer view of Luke's face. He is breathing hard. Not from exertion, but from anger. His eyes are hard with hatred, and show a hunger for blood. He is stiff, his muscles tense. He places his daggers back into his belt. Then, closing his eyes, he begins to change.

Luke hunches over, his black clothing melting into his body. His hands become claws. A tail forms and twitches. Cap takes a step back, surprised and shocked. Luke opens his eyes, and Cap finds himself staring into the blue eyes of a huge panther. Cap's mouth drops in surprise, not believing or wanting to believe that this is his brother.

"Surprised?" Luke growls, "I told you we aren't brothers any longer."

Cap's mouth remains open in shock. He wasn't expecting this. The shock of it refuses to wear off. He is frozen. His head tells him to do or say anything, but his muscles aren't listening. Luke's muscles tense and twitch, and he pounces at Cap. The twitching is just enough. Cap comes out of his trance just in time to lift his shield. Luke hit's the shield hard, knocking Cap to the ground. Luke lands on his feet, turns and leaps for

Cap's throat.

Cap, still on the ground, manages to get Adflictus' shaft up, the cat's teeth clamping down on it. Pain flows throughout his body as Luke's claws pierce his skin. He can feel his clothing getting wet with blood. Getting his feet under the cat, he pushes up, throwing Luke over his head. Luke lands on his side, rolls over and gets up quickly. Cap stands, trying to ignore the pain. Luke circles around Cap slowly. He dashes in, and jumps. Instead of jumping high like Cap expected, he goes low, grazing he outside Cap's thigh with his claw. Clothing tears and skin and blood are exposed.

Cap hits his knees with the new pain. Luke smiles in his panther form. Jumping at Cap from behind, his hind legs land on Cap's shoulders and tear into his muscles. Cap yells out in pain. Luke continues to circle, toying with his prey.

"The all mighty Cap," Luke growls with sarcasm, "Defeats the zombie army single handedly. Defender and aggressor. Can take on vampires and werecats with little effort. The hero Cap, now at the mercy of a single foe." He laughs evilly, "It is ironic, isn't it? Your demise won't be from a fight, but by refusing one."

Cap stands up very slowly. His vision brightens with the now familiar red tint. "I won't fight back," he tells Luke, "but you cannot defeat me."

Luke snarls, and leaps. Cap sidesteps, tapping the cat's back with Adflictus lightly. Luke lands on his feet, and lets out a roar from being insulted. He walks in close to Cap. Cap has his arms open, inviting Luke to attack. The cat slashes with its paws. Cap dodges, each slash missing by inches. Luke tries to bite at Cap, but Cap steps back and laughs.

Luke, angry at the insult in such a way, pounces again. His forepaws are out, waiting for Cap to throw up his shield to block. Instead, Cap drops his weapon, and grabs the paws of the werecat. Holding him up,

Luke is forced to look Cap in the eyes. He snaps at Cap's face, but he is too far away. Cap doesn't flinch. Luke's hind paws tear at the ground, trying to get fee. Cap's strength is greater than he expected though. Suddenly filled with fear, he bites at Cap's arm. Cap releases the paw, and Luke pulls free from his grip.

Luke backs out of Cap's reach, even though Cap doesn't make a move towards him. Luke circles around Cap. Cap doesn't move, allowing Luke to get behind him. Luke jumps at his back. With swift speed, Cap turns out of the way, grabbing Luke by the ribs and setting him down on the ground. Luke turns quickly and swipes, but he only slices the air. Cap is already out of reach, waiting for him.

"Fight!" Luke roars angrily.

Cap laughs, "Sure. Just as soon as there is someone worthy of fighting."

Luke roars again, and attacks Cap once more. He slashes, pounces, and bites with speed he didn't know he had. Yet, it isn't enough. Cap is able to move out of the way of all of it. Luke continues to attack, more hopeful for a lucky blow than a clean hit. Cap continues to dodge it all, still refusing to fight.

Luke backs up, panting with exhaustion. His eyes are cold and hard. His muscles are getting weary. He stares at Cap, contemplating on how to get at him. He moves too quickly for a normal strike, and he isn't weak. This makes it very difficult to fight close. Luke sniffs the air. He can smell Cap's blood. The scent makes him salivate.

He looks Cap up and down again. His clothes are torn. He is bleeding steadily where Luke's claws had penetrated. He is breathing heavy, although he is trying to hide it. Cap is tensed up, yet he's having trouble keeping his arms up to guard attacks. Luke smiles with a mean snarl. He is winning. He only has to win this battle of endurance.

Movement behind Cap catches his eye. Looking behind his enemy, he can see a large group of vampires moving stealthily behind Cap. He continues to watch as they begin to hide themselves in the tall grass. He circles around as the vampires hide out of sight. He stops when he knows they are at his back. He returns back to his human form.

"You've lost," Luke states.

"Not even close," Cap responds.

Luke laughs. Cap's face gets a confused shade across it. Worry wipes away his confusion as Breanna walks up beside Luke. Now he has a serious problem. He is in no shape to fight Breanna, and dodge Luke's attacks. If they attack simultaneously, it will be very difficult to defend against. He takes a deep breath, and reassures himself. He cannot lose. He must not lose.

"You've caused me a lot of trouble," Breanna says to him.

"You're welcome," Cap says, picking up his weapon and preparing himself for defense.

"I had thought of letting you live," she says angrily, "but now, the only end can be death for you."

"I'm ready," he says, getting Adflictus into position.

Breanna smiles meanly. "We'll see," she says, and looks over her shoulder, "Now!" she orders. A group of vampires rises into the air, bows and arrows in their hands, ready to fire.

Cap's eyes get wide as the arrows are released. He hits the ground, knees at his chest. He covers what he can of his chest with his shield. The sound of arrows deflecting off of his shield, helmet, and leg armor echoes through the air. The sound doesn't seem to end. Then it is mixed with his own yell of agony as arrows land in his feet and the uncovered parts of his legs.

The assault ends, and he uncovers himself to find the arrows still embedded in his flesh. He looks at Luke and Breanna as he pulls them out. They both are smiling greedily. Using Adflictus, he pushes himself off the ground, wincing with pain. Forcing himself to balance, he gets back into a fighting stance.

Breanna and Luke rush at the same time. Cap manages to block Breanna's attack, but misses Luke's. Luke's dagger slices his flesh by his ribs, and he lands on his knees with pain. He forces himself back to his feet, determined not to give up. Breanna and Luke are on opposite sides of him now. They attack again, and he is unable to block either. He is spun around, and lands hard. The taste of blood enters his mouth, and he finds himself in a mud puddle of his own blood.

He tries to get up again. As he pulls himself to his knees, he looks up to see Luke standing above him. Luke kicks him in the head, knocking him to the ground. Breathing in gasps, Cap tries to roll over. Luke kicks him in the ribs, and pushes down on Cap's chest with his foot. Cap pushes Luke's foot away, but Luke kicks him again and presses down harder.

"You should have fought," Luke tells him, "You could have won. Now, the Great Cap will fall." He raises his dagger above his head, and thrusts down at Cap.

Time seems to slow down as Cap watches the dagger. The dagger gets to Luke's hip, and something happens. Cap is suddenly falling! Still looking up, he watches Luke trip and fall to the side of a hole. Cap looks around him, and notices that he is falling into the ground! Looking up again, he watches the ground close in above him. He can hear Luke screaming in disbelief as the hole closes and light fades away.

Panicking, Cap tries to grab a hold of something, anything! His hands find nothing but air. His feet hit something, slip, and he lands on his tail bone. Wincing with pain, he now feels himself sliding downwards. He looks down, and sees a small light. The light grows bigger as he gets closer.

Afraid of what might be at the end, he tries to slow himself down, but he only slides faster.

The ground tears at his clothing and skin. The light has become a tunnel, and he can see that it ends at a cliff. Again he tries to stop, but the slide gets steeper, and he is unable to. The ground fattens out, and he slides off of the cliff. He feels weightless as he is suspended in the air. Above, he can see the roof of a cave. Wind whips by as he falls down. He lands with a thud, his breath knocked out of him. He rolls to his side, trying to breathe again.

Cool moist air fills his lungs suddenly, and he opens his eyes in relief. He notices that he is in front of a city. He is too weary to think about it though. Lying on his back, he breathes very heavily. He closes his eyes. Shadows appear through his eyelids.

"Welcome to Agartha," he hears a man's voice say.

'It isn't over,' Cap thinks, with hope and resolve as his conscious fades away, 'It isn't over yet.'

Agartha, an ancient city that resides deep within the ground. It is a magnificent city, with remnants of an ancient and advanced culture. The buildings rise like tall skyscrapers. Although, they have many more curves. The city is lighted by a white energy orb that can only be compared to a large electric light bulb. It is truly a city of many hidden technologies. No one from the top of Immortalis has ever seen it. No one from the city has ever been top side. The stranger's arrival is causing both controversy and worry.

The town has been secluded, not interacting with the societies above. Rumors and debates spread like wild fire. Why is the strange man here? How did he get here? What is his purpose? Is he an enemy, or a friend? These answers should be answered soon by the council. What is taking them so long?

All the while, the truth of the matter is the council is procrastinating their meeting. This has never happened before, and they are not sure what to think of it either. It is extremely unexpected, and none of the council members doubt that another will share the same views. Each member is preparing for a large debate among the ten seats.

At the council building, two men wait for news about the stranger. He has been terribly wounded, and is receiving medical care as they wait. They wait not only to find out about him, but to make their decisions afterwards. Of the two, one has already made up his mind.

"Councilman Butukhan? Is it wise to keep the stranger with us?" the younger of the two asks, "We do not know who he is. Let alone what his intentions may be."

"You would have let him die on the ground, Councilman Bat?" Butukhan asks in return, "No. No matter what his intentions may be, we are not killers. We do not judge those we know not about. We did the right thing. Our conscious is clear."

"It is dangerous to keep a man from the topside here," Bat argues, "Our way of life could be in jeopardy."

"Then we will have to wait and see how he fares," Butukhan replies.

"That may not happen as soon as we would like," a female says, walking up to them, "He has lost a lot of blood, and I'm not sure our medicine will help him."

"Councilwoman Saransatsaral," Butukhan greets her, "I'm pleased that you could join us. How could our medicine not help him? Unless his injuries are more terminal?"

"That's the odd thing," she responds, "We can't tell. He's lost a lot of blood, and may have some internal injuries along with the other injuries we've found. It is up to fate and his own will to survive, that will determine if he lives or not. If he does survive, there is no telling how long he will be unconscious or be able to recover. It could be hours, days, or even weeks!"

"That should make the decision easier," Bat says.

"Hardly," Butukhan says to him, "I believe that makes our decision harder. Save your arguments for the meeting. We should begin with indifference, and no influence. Our minds need to be clear before we decide any man's fate." Butukhan looks down the street to see the rest of the council walking towards them, "Let us head inside. We will begin shortly."

They walk into the building and into a room labeled in the ancient language. The room is small and plain. There are no decorations in the room, except for the ancient language trimming the ceiling. Nine white cushioned chairs make a half circle around a small podium. Butukhan waits against the wall, staring at the small chandelier hanging from the ceiling.

Bat and Saransatsral take their seats in the center as the rest of the council enters. They talk quietly among themselves as Butukhan walks up to the podium.

"If everyone will be seated, please," he calls out to everyone in the room, "I now call this emergency session of the council to order. We all know why we are here. We shouldn't waste any time. I now leave the floor open for arguments."

"We should be rid of the stranger," Bat says immediately, "He is a threat to us, and our way of life."

"How could you be so cruel?" Saransatsral asks him, "He is injured and alone. We should take care of him and provide sanctuary. What do you think, Councilman Narambaatar?" she asks an elderly gentleman to her right.

"Normally I would agree with you," Narambaatar says to her, "but something is amiss topside. The feeling I'm getting is that the stranger is a big part of it."

"Exactly," Councilwoman Bayarnaa says from the far left side, "Let those who live above stay above."

"You think he arrived voluntarily?" Councilman Chuluun asks from beside Narambaatar, "No one knows those ancient entrances. Not up top, or down below."

"That's not the point!" Councilman Sukhbataar yells from the far right, "He is here now. He now knows how to get here. He is a threat, and he must be dealt with!"

Councilwoman Odval yells back from the seat next to Sukhbataar, "He fell through the ancient cave. Only a higher power could have brought him to us!"

"For what purpose?" Councilwoman Khongordzat asks from the seat next to Bat, "If it is not coincidence, why *is* he here?"

"The only way to find out is to help him recover from his wounds," Councilwoman Bolormas says from beside Khongordzat, "If we get rid of him, we will never know."

Bat stands up angrily, "What about this is so difficult? It is far too dangerous to keep him here!"

Odval stands up just as angrily to respond, "Do you have no sense of decency? We cannot let a helpless man die just because we are afraid. That is immoral! We cannot allow ourselves to be ruled by such fears!"

"Fear is what has kept our society alive," Naranbaatar says, "It isn't out of the question."

"I can't believe all of you!" Chuluun exclaims, "This isn't a rabid dog we are talking about, he is a human being! He is no different than us!"

"Agreed," Saransatsral says, "He is here and he can't leave on his own. You should be ashamed of yourselves for thinking he could do us any harm!"

"Because he could lead enemies from topside down to us!" Sukhbaatar yells at her, "If enemies could follow him down here, we could all be in grave danger!"

"And that's what scares you?" Bolormas asks, "Are you afraid for the lives of the people? Or your own?"

Everyone begins yelling and screaming at each other. Butukhan just steps back and lets them go at it. If it were up to him alone, the stranger would have the medical attention that he needs, and sanctuary until he is better. At the least until he was well enough to travel on his own. There are many tunnels and secret paths leading out of town. It is possible that he could find a way back to the top, or even get lost. However, there is a curiosity within him that wants to know. He would like to know how he received his injuries, and what his purpose is. His destiny may involve the people of Agartha somehow, or may not. What purpose he is here for, though, or even how he acquired his injuries is irrelevant.

He is brought back from his thoughts by Bat's voice. "I motion we vote now!" Bat says above the noise.

"I second that motion!" Bayarma yells before anyone can argue.

The members quiet down, many with faces red with anger. They all sit as paper is passed around for the vote. It is customary to have secret ballots on controversial issues. This vote is no different. None of the council members want their names out in public if they were to make the wrong decision. Their careers could be over if that information was ever released.

The silence is interrupted by the door slamming open. They all turn to see the stranger limping slowly with a crutch under his left arm into the room. He is naked from the waste up, except for the blood soaked bandages around his abdomen and shoulders. Behind him follow two nurses, pleading with him to return to his room and to bed. The stranger pays them no mind. He continues forward, walking to the podium.

"I apologize to the council," one of the nurses says, "He woke and learned about the meeting. He wouldn't be stopped."

Butukhan looks at the stranger, now standing in front of him. He can't help but admire the man's determination. The stranger is sweating profusely, and his bandages look soaked with fresh blood. Probably from the exertion of walking. He is breathing hard, but his eyes show not fatigue, but determination. The man is on a mission and will not be stopped. Butukhan smiles at him. Here they were, not sure if he would survive, and now the man stands before them for everyone to see. Not only did he survive, but managed to muster the strength to come to this very meeting. Butukhan can't hide the admiration in his eyes at the thought.

"It is fine," Butukhan tells the nurses, "but stay close." He looks back at the stranger, "You, sir, should remain in bed until you have healed."

"If my fate is to be decided, I have the right to be present," the stranger says sternly, "Also, I would like to address this council before you make a decision."

"The motion has been seconded," Bat calls out, "Let the vote proceed!"

Butukhan doesn't acknowledge Bat. "Can you handle it?" he asks the stranger, "You don't look well."

"I'll live," the stranger says to him, "I can handle it."

Butukhan nods his head, and addresses the council, "He will speak before we vote. Please, remain silent while he speaks." He moves to the side to allow the stranger room.

The stranger gets behind the podium, places both hands on top of it for balance, and speaks very clearly, "My name is Casey 'Cap' Cenere. I prefer to be called Cap, but that isn't the discussion you are having today. I am not from here, or from the lands above. I have been brought here none the less. I have the titles of both Commander of Avalon and General of the combined forces of the Greeks, Celts, and Norse. I don't know if you are aware, but a war has begun in the lands above. I'm not going to ask for much. I just want to get back up top as soon as possible. I need to be beside my friends, and fight with my men. Besides that, my fate rests in your hands."

Cap leaves the podium, and limps over to the wall. He leans against it, pushing the nurses trying to tend to him away. Butukhan smiles at the sight. How a man that badly injured can keep two nurses at bay boggles the mind. The man must be a great warrior. He has strength inside, much more than shows outside. That instant, with that one thought, Butukhan makes up his mind about what will happen to this man's fate.

Stepping behind the podium again, he addresses the council, "Let the vote proceed. In accordance with tradition, and our laws, a two thirds majority will end this session."

The council members begin writing on their personal ballots. They seem to take turns looking at Cap. He doesn't seem to notice, but stares at the podium. One by one they take their votes up to the podium. Butukhan looks at each one, tallies it, and then places it inside a ceramic jar. After the last ballot is placed in the jar, he pours a liquid in it and shakes it up. He then takes it to the door and hands it to a servant waiting outside.

He returns to the podium, and looks at the tally sheet. "Are there any objections to the vote?" he asks them. No one answers, so he continues, "By a vote of seven to three, the stranger Cap, will stay with us. We will provide sanctuary, and whatever else he needs to recover."

"That can't be!" Bat exclaims.

"That was the vote," Sarantsatsral says proudly, "It shall be done."

Bat's face gets red with anger. Butukhan remains at the podium, hiding his own emotions. He is very happy with the way it had all turned out. The rest of the council has looks of worry. They don't know what will happen next, and they worry mostly about that. Cap remains against the wall, a small smile upon his face. He doesn't make a sound, but his presence seems to radiate through the small room.

Butukhan calls out through the room, "The vote is a two thirds majority. This emergency session of the council is closed." He walks over to Cap as everyone else leaves the room. He waves off the nurses, wanting to talk to Cap alone.

"The vote wasn't seven to three, was it?" Cap asks after they are alone.

"Why would you think that?" Butukhan asks back.

"You didn't look at half of the ballets," Cap responds, "That could be dangerous for you."

"You don't miss much, do you?" Butukhan asks laughing, looking at him hesitantly.

"It is becoming a bad habit," Cap replies, humor in his voice.

"Well, let me walk you back to your room."

Cap laughs, "Don't you mean, 'Let me help in case you collapse'?"

Butukhan laughs also, "Yeah, you don't miss much at all." Cap just shrugs his shoulders.

They walk out of the building, and to the street. Cap turns to walk down it, but Butukhan stops him. Coming up the street is a long wheeled vehicle. No animals are pulling it, but it isn't an automobile either. It is very curvy, and low to the ground. Cap tries to look beneath it without falling over, looking for tires underneath it. Try as he might, he cannot see any.

"What is it?" Cap asks.

Butukhan smiles with pride, "The ancients called it a mobilno. We've been using them for many millennia."

"We have something similar at home," Cap says, "We call ours cars."

Butukhan's pride seems to fade away, "Technology has caught up where you are from?"

"And surpassed it, I think," Cap tells him, getting into the vehicle, "We can communicate over long distances in an instant. We have information at our fingertips whenever we want it. Vehicles that fly, and some that travel underground. We have even managed to get a selected few to walk on the moon!"

"Then humanity *has* caught up! According to the archives, it didn't seem like any civilization ever would."

"That was thousands of years ago," Cap says, "I'm sure much was lost in the war with Atlantis."

"You know about that?!" Butukhan asks surprised.

Cap closes his eyes, "Agartha. The remnant city of Lemuria. Sole surviving city when the kingdoms of Atlantis and Lemuria destroyed each other in a war long, long ago." He opens his eyes, "It isn't well known, but the story goes that the war destroyed technologies of both societies."

"I'm impressed," Butukhan says as the vehicle stops.

"Now I have a couple questions," Cap says, "I know why I can understand your language, but how can you understand mine?"

"You've taken a potion, or had a spell cast upon you?" Butukhan asks. Cap nods his head yes, so Butukhan explains, "Than you don't notice that you speak with an accent. When you are talking to someone that doesn't speak the same language as you, you speak in their tongue. You can understand all languages, but what you don't realize is that you are speaking different languages to different people. It is more complicated than what it sounds like."

"That explains a lot," Cap says, "Next question. I noticed an underground river to the south of town from my room. Where does it flow?"

"No one really knows," Butukhan answers, "Leaving the city is forbidden. Rumors have circulated that it goes to Atlantis, but that is only rumors."

"Well, let's hope it is a way out of here," Cap says hopefully, "I need to be on my way as soon as I can. My enemies will find a way here if they think I'm still alive."

"Nobody knows the entrances here," Butukhan says confidently, reassuring Cap. He is about to say something else, then stops suddenly.

"Except?" Cap asks.

"Except Cronus," Butukhan answers, "He is the creator, he knows. He sent a messenger here a few days before you arrived. He wanted to know if he could have our assistance."

"You need to get me out of here immediately," Cap tells him.

"You aren't healthy enough to travel!"

"It is me or the city. If they even think you are assisting me, they will come and tear the town apart."

"That's impossible," Butukhan says in disbelief.

"As impossible as me falling through a nonexistent hole in the ground and landing here? Nothing is impossible, only improbable," Cap explains to him, "If you want to stay isolated and out of the conflict, you need to send me on my way."

"So be it," Butukhan agrees with reluctance, "I'll have a ship built for you to travel on the river. Until then, you can remain here and recuperate. I'll have someone come and repair your clothing for you also."

"Thank you, that is too much though," Cap says gratefully.

"I would also like to hear your story, if there is time," Butukhan says.

"I can tell it to you while we wait," Cap replies, "but what if they come after me before I can leave? Or after?"

"If anything is brought to the city, with or without you here, we will not hesitate about sending our own forces topside and waging war. You have come to us under extenuating circumstances, and in peace. You mean us no harm, nor have you shown any aggression towards us. We must give you sanctuary," Butukhan smiles very humorously, "After all, it was a two thirds majority."

Chapter 22

Celebration throughout El Dorado continues on. The successful rescue of Diamondback has given everyone renewed hope. The week long fiesta is finally coming to an end. Never before has the city seen such a celebration. Tonight, everyone anticipates the music and dancing that will soon occur. Well, almost everyone.

Isabella, Salma, Athena, Aphrodite, Logan, and Adolf all sit in an office silently. To them, the success of Cap's mission is worth the fiesta, along with his other feats. On the other hand, he is missing, and the loss is being felt by everyone. Especially by all those that have befriended him. They are the ones who feel the loss the most.

They have tried to find him. When the news came that both Breanna and Luke were upset at losing Cap, Isabella ordered groups in every direction to search for him. Adolf had even snuck into Avalon among the werecats to find out what happened. When he returned, he confirmed that the story was true. During the fight, the ground swallowed Cap. It happened at the most inopportune time. Luke and Breanna were both shocked and appalled at what had happened. What could have happened to him though, is anyone's guess.

After days of searching, they all began to give up hope. Though everyone is happy to have Diamondback again, the mood remains very somber. Only the select few remain worried. Without Cap, how will they be able to defend against the Vampiric Army? Let alone, defeat it. Cap has become their leader, their savior. He has given the people hope, strength, and courage. His loss will be devastating to the moral of the land.

The six of them sit silent, dwelling on the thoughts in their heads. No one notices the servant walking into the room.

"Governor," the servant says quietly, "It is time."

Isabella nods her head in acknowledgement. She stands up, and leaves the room with everyone following her. The streets are empty as she walks to the plaza. The citizens and soldiers mingle together as she enters the area. Everyone seems to have a cheery disposition. If she didn't know better, Isabella would think that Cap missing didn't bother them. It does though. The feeling is in the air.

The crowd silences as she walks onto the stage. Everyone in the plaza begins to gather in front of the stage. Behind her, the musicians tune their instruments. Standing in the middle of the stage, Isabella contemplates what she will say to the crowd in front of her. She had a speech prepared, but it feels out of place now. The sound of pure silence lets her know that her contemplation time is up.

"On this night," she begins, speaking plainly and loudly, "This night we celebrate with great enthusiasm. Our final night to be thankful for all of our heroes who have sacrificed so much. All gave some, and yet some gave all. We cannot allow that to bring our spirits down though. We must celebrate for them. For if it wasn't for all they have done for us, we would not be here this night.

"Many times we take what we have for granted. We allow chance and fate to determine the direction our lives will take. Most of the time, that is enough. Yet, times have changed. No longer can we allow ourselves to be led by chance. No longer can we be manipulated by a false sense of fate. The decisions are in front of us. It is up to each and every one of us to choose. The decisions we make from now on will affect everyone in the future. We must make these choices with pride. We must face fate with happiness, and not fear. We celebrate that tonight.

"So this night, take great pride in the defenders of our freedom. Celebrate the lives of those who took fate into their own hands. Smile at those who choose to sacrifice themselves for the greater good. Most of all, never forget. Always remember those lost. The missing and the fallen. Celebrate for them. For it is they who deserve our gratitude most of all. They are the ones who have earned our trust and respect. It is they, above all others, who deserve our gratitude."

The crowd begins to applaud as Isabella walks off of the stage. The band replaces her, and begins to play. She stands silently on the side. Her appearance solidifying her feelings to the crowd. Though she may not be a soldier or a warrior, there are many things she can do to help. Keeping moral high, for her anyway, seems to be the high priority. That she can try to do. Providing supplies is another. That is the most simple, and most important act of anything she can do.

Looking up at the sky, she notices the imps flying into the plaza. A feeling of worry overwhelms her. The people haven't quite accepted them as part of their own. True to Cap's word though, they have treated the imps with respect. The imps land and begin dancing to the music. To Isabella's delight, the people begin dancing with them. Tonight, it seems, is a time for tolerance and acceptance. Everyone is equal, and no one is considered less than another.

"It is good to see," Salma says, startling Isabella, "Everyone is happy. Your speech touched the hearts of everyone."

"I was only speaking the truth," Isabella tells her.

"Yes," Salma responds, "and it is well overdue. It is something to think about. If it weren't for Cap, I think we would all continue believing that fate will guide our actions. He has brought a new way of thinking to us all."

"And he is missed the most," Isabella says sadly, "He is followed by everyone. With him gone, I wonder if we will stay unified."

Diamondback walks up to them from the crowd, "I think we can. We just need to believe in what he stood for. Nice speech, by the way."

"Thanks," Isabella answers, "but what do you mean?"

"Think about it," he says, "He fights for a land not his own. He demands respect, for others more than himself. He has asked for nothing, and he was willing to sacrifice himself for his friends, particularly me. These aren't qualities you will find in the average person on the street. They are very rare, and almost everyone loves him for it. We can believe while he is gone. We can honor him by believing and in doing so, stay together."

"It is a good thought," Salma says.

A guard comes running up to them, "Governor! There is a werecat at the west gate. He demands to speak to who is in charge."

Isabella's face gets grave, "Are you sure?"

"Yes, ma'am," the guard says. He turns and runs, Isabella running behind him.

The streets look like death they are so empty. With everyone at the dance, it looks like only ghosts reside here. The lamps left on in the empty houses light the streets very eerily. Running through the shadows, Isabella can't help but feel a little scared about who she is about to meet. 'A male werecat?' she thinks, 'There isn't any male werecats that rank that high in Cronus' army. Not one, except...'

Running up the stairway to the wall's ramparts, she gets a view of who the werecat is. Luke stands in front of the gate. He is difficult to see in his dark clothing. Half a dozen bows are drawn and aimed at him. He doesn't seem fazed, however. He just stands there smiling, his white smile contrasting with his clothing.

Isabella takes a deep breath, calming herself for the conversation ahead. "You wanted to see me, Luke?" she asks.

"I asked for who was in charge," he answers, "I never thought it would be you. This could be fun."

"Don't get too excited," Adolf says walking out of the shadows behind Luke, "She isn't alone."

"Ah," Luke says, not looking back, "a pet. Listen, I came alone and in peace to deliver a message. Keep the dog where he's at, but lower the bows. They won't do much to me anyways."

Isabella hesitates. She looks at the archers to her right, they are looking at her. She can see Logan sneaking up to her on the ramparts, so she nods at the archers who lower their bows. She turns her head back to Luke, "Alright, deliver your message."

Luke continues to smile, "Breanna wants you to know that we know where Cap is, and only we will be able to get him. Forget any hope of seeing him again. That is unless you agree with us."

"And what is it she wants us to agree to?" she asks.

"She wants to end this war once and for all. A final battle between our forces and yours," he says.

"Is she suicidal?" Isabella asks surprised, "She has been outmatched twice already. Is she ready for a third?"

"That was with Cap!" Luke yells, suddenly angry, "Plus, we have some new recruits. Recruits that hate and despise your forces. You've heard of the Great Persian Army? Well they have all joined us. That is an army larger than all of your forces combined! Plus all the werecats and vampires."

His smile reappears, "She is going to give you two nights after tonight. If you don't show, we will destroy El Dorado. We will burn every village, kill every person, and turn any who try to flee. From here to New Athens, we will destroy everything. That is your choice, of course, if you would call it one."

Isabella feels her face get red with anger, "Where at? Where does she want our armies to meet?"

Luke's smile widens, "The south sea, just north of the delta. Two days, and two nights time. Now, if you will call off your dog, I'll be on my way. Remember, two nights." Luke looks back at Adolf as the werewolf backs away. He turns and disappears into the shadows.

Isabella grabs the nearest guard, "Get me Cuchulain, Heracles, and Sir Palomedes now! There is no time to waste!"

As the guard runs to look for the two heroes and the knight, Isabella turns her attention into the darkness. All of a sudden, she doesn't want to be governor any longer. The decisions being forced upon her are weighing heavily on her heart. She shakes her head, shaking off the pessimism. She must prevail. *They* must prevail. Not only for the sake of all the innocent lives of Immortalis, but for the memory of Cap also. She shakes her head again. Now isn't the time to think about all that. Now is the time to prepare for battle.

Chapter 23

Diamondback stands with Cuchulain, Sir Palomedes and Heracles. They stand silently staring at the massive Persian army across the field in the light of the full moon. It took them two days and one night to arrive, but they made it on time. Their armies are tired and weary, and he fears that they won't be able to survive the battle ahead. The sheer size of the Persian army alone has to be at least fifty thousand strong. They are insurmountable odds for the ten thousand they have with them. From where they stand, the eastern horizon is amassed with soldiers as far as the eye can see. It will be a miracle if anyone survives the night.

Diamondback feels his pulse. It is beating rapidly from his nervousness. His heart feels like it is about to explode from his chest. He had volunteered to take Cap's place. No one else would at the time. Now, it seems, he should have let someone more capable take over. He has never commanded a force like this. There is no way he can be positive about what to do. What worries him the most is that he doesn't see the vampires. He constantly catches himself looking back, worried that they will attack from behind.

Those worries fade away as the Vampiric Army floats into sight. They land behind the Persians, with the werecats. Now, he is really worried. He looks all around himself. All the men have the same look of fear in their eyes that he feels. Even the two great heroes tremble with fear for a moment, but quickly gain their composure. He can feel himself shake with fear as he looks across the field.

Breanna, Martine, and Luke move to the front of the forces, and walk out to the empty field. Diamondback, Sir Palomedes, Cuchulain, and Heracles do the same, although slower to give their men some more time to recover. Breanna and Luke both look angry and irritated. Something must have gone wrong. Diamondback can only hope it is for their benefit. If it isn't, may God have mercy on all their souls.

"Something is wrong," Cuchulain says suddenly.

"What?" Diamondback asks him.

"Look at the sky," Cuchulain answers.

"It is a crystal clear night," Heracles says, "What about it?"

"Exactly," Cuchulain replies, "There is about to be a major battle, and the sky is clear. Something is wrong. Look at them," Cuchulain nods towards their three counterparts, "They know it too."

Diamondback looks at his three adversaries. Their faces stay focused forward, but their eyes move up to the sky and back down again. They are worried about it! This could be a good thing. There may be some way of taking advantage of this. How though, he has no idea. He just hopes that something will come to him before it is too late.

The seven commanders meet in the middle of the field. They stare at each other, measuring each other in turn. Breanna, Martine, and Luke have the upper hand, their combined forces being larger than any ever seen in Immortalis. The three heroes, on the other hand, have the single advantage. Their weaknesses are far different, and less severe as their adversaries. However, this won't be a singles battle. There lies the problem for them…maybe.

Sir Palomedes speaks first, "You walked out first. What terms are you offering?"

Breanna smiles very coldly, "We would like to make you an offer."

"Which is?" Heracles asks.

"You surrender your armies to us," Martine tells them, "and swear fealty to Cronus. In return, you will all stay commanders of your forces. We will only want a small percentage of your men for our own uses."

"And if we refuse?" Diamondback asks.

"Total annihilation," Luke says, "We won't allow a man one to leave this field alive."

"Hmm, interesting," is all Sir Palomedes says.

"I suppose you have terms of your own?" Breanna asks.

"Yes," Diamondback says, "Walk your forces off of this field. No one will die, everyone will live, and you can tell Cronus where to shove-"

"Diamondback!" Cuchulain yells, "This isn't the time or the place."

"Give us a minute to discuss the details of your proposal," Sir Palomedes says. Breanna nods her head in agreement, and the three men huddle around each other.

"We can't surrender our men to them," Heracles whispers.

"We won't be able to win a victory either," Sir Palomedes responds, "With our armies gone, Immortalis will be virtually defenseless!"

"Even more so if we agree to their terms," Diamondback says.

"What would Cap do?" Cuchulain asks.

"He would do what he thinks is right," Diamondback answers, "but he isn't here. I know what I would do though."

"What would that be?" asks Heracles.

"I'd fight. If I'm goin' down, it won't be without a fight. And I'm damn sure that I'm takin' a whole hell of a lot of 'em with me."

"I think we all feel that way," Cuchulain says to them, "But we have more than ourselves to think about here."

"Then what should we do?" Diamondback asks them.

Heracles looks down at the ground, then into Diamondback's eyes very seriously, "The decision is yours. You took over command. We'll follow your choice," he pauses for a moment, smiling conspicuously, "to an extent, of course."

Diamondback looks at the armies that followed them here. The front line looks restless and nervous. Right then, the realization hits him that they came for one reason. To end this war. To fight for those who don't have the ability to fight. To not back down when the odds are stacked against them, but to make the odds their very own. They didn't follow because they had to. They followed because they chose to. These men, these very brave men, are here to fight for their beliefs. It doesn't matter that the man next to him may believe in something different. To give up would be giving up their beliefs, families, and livelihoods. They came to win, and they aren't going to go down without a fight. He knows what he has to do now. Even though he knows what the outcome may be.

"How 'bout this," Diamondback says smiling as he turns around, "We don't surrender. We don't swear fealty. We will not give you any percentage of our men. Let's decide to march these armies off the field, and we all live to fight another day."

"There is no negotiation here!" Luke yells walking up to Diamondback, "You agree or you don't. Is that too hard for you to understand, freak!?"

Diamondback punches Luke in the mouth, knocking him to the ground. "Kiss my ass you pathetic little fur ball! You wanna settle this right? Then let's go! Man to man! If that's too much for you, you puny little piss ant, then walk off the field like the coward you are! Come on! Get up! Let's go! One on one! Just you and me!"

"ENOUGH!" Breanna yells, "Do you agree or not?"

"GO TO HELL!" Diamondback yells back, his face red with anger.

"Then you choose death," Breanna says as Luke picks himself off the ground, "So be it." They turn around, and walk back to their forces.

Heracles and Cuchulain almost drag Diamondback back to their lines. Diamondback is almost frothing at the mouth, ready to fight and no longer nervous. All he sees and wants is blood now. As far as he is concerned, death awaits anyone who gets in his way. A gust of cold wind hits him from the south. He turns to look, still red with anger. Lightning flashes as the wind grows stronger.

The waves along the sea begin to hit the shore very hard, giving an ominous sound to the upcoming battle. A forceful wind begins to blow from the south sea. Both forces look towards the water to see numerous sails on the horizon. They grow quickly, moving towards the shoreline with exceptional speed. All anyone can do is watch as the ships reach the shore. Another gust of wind pushes the ships, and the sea, right up the southern line of Diamondback's forces. On the flagship, front and center of all of them, stands Cap. Standing beside him is a man in a white robe and a man in a green toga.

Cap jumps down, followed by the two strange men. The armies of Immortalis roar with enthusiasm at seeing their general alive and well. Armies and machines unload quickly from the ships. Cap walks up to the Heracles, Sir Palomedes, Cuchulain, and Diamondback. He shakes each man's hand in turn, and then looks behind them at the army.

"Damn," Diamondback says with both surprise and relief, "Am I glad to see you."

"Nice to see you too," Cap responds, "What have I missed?"

"Just the usual," Sir Palomedes says, "Breanna demanding surrender, asking for men for their uses, offering us our lives and survival. You know, the usual."

"And Diamondback knocking your brother to the ground," Heracles half chuckles. "And that," he says more seriously, pointing across the field.

"Oh good God!" Cap exclaims.

"Yeah," Cuchulain agrees, "Even with the army you brought with you, we are still outnumbered. I'm not sure there can be a victory for us."

"Oh ye of little faith," Cap says smiling, "I'd like you to meet Butukhan of Agartha," he says pointing to the man in the white robe, "And Anastasios of Atlantis," he points to the man in the green toga, "They are here to help."

"How did you-" Heracles half asks, very confused.

"Let's just say Cronus and Breanna tried to extend their reach a little too far in way too many places," Cap tells them, "I'll explain later. What do you have planned for the battle?"

"Pray that our men can fight through that army, and then follow through with it. Hopefully killing all of them," Diamondback tells him, "I'm really hoping that you have something better in mind."

Cap smiles, then turns to Butukhan and Anastasios, "Can your artillery stop theirs, and their arrows also?"

"Easily," Butukhan says, "Allow us to deal with their artillery."

"Then we will take the archers and arrows," Anastasios says, "Feel free to take those out of your scenario."

"Good!" Cap says, "Now, here's what I want us to do. I want my men, the knights, and the Norse army with me in the center of the line. Staggered back to my right, Cuchulain and his army. Staggered behind them, the Agarthan army. To my left I want Heracles and his army staggered the same way, followed by the Atlantean army. We will march onto the field in that formation. My force will take point. Let them push us back. As they get closer to you, begin moving forward and assaulting their flanks. I'll continue to fall back. As soon as I get behind the Agarthans and Atlanteans, close in. Leave them no escape. Take them all out.

"Now, are the imps here?"

"They are behind the lines," Cuchulain answers him.

"Send a messenger. Tell them to get started." Cap orders, "We'll need all their help immediately. Where are Adolf and Logan?"

"They went to gather the werewolf packs," Diamondback answers him, "We don't know if they will make it in time."

"No time to worry about that then," Cap says disappointed, "Let's get moving," he points to the Persian army, "They won't wait for us."

Cap walks to the front center as the commanders scatter to their forces. The water begins to recede back south to the sea, taking the ships with it. As the Avalon soldiers, knights, and the Norse army line up in ranks beside Cap, the Persian army releases their artillery. Boulders and gigantic jars of fire fly towards them. With the sounds of light explosions, white bursts take out each projectile flying towards them, then the artillery and every soldier manning it.

Cap can hear orders in anger from across the field as he watches arrows fly into the air. The amount of arrows are so many, they almost block the light of the moon. As darkness surrounds them, a green light shoots out above them. It fans out across the sky. As the arrows penetrate the light, they fall to the ground as ash. While the final arrow burns to the ground, the light bends. Screams of terror and pain sound across the field as the archers are burned alive.

Cap turns around to address his army, "Tonight is the night we decide the future of Immortalis! We will either find a way to victory, or make one of our own!" He turns around, raising Adflictus high into the air and yells, "We finish this tonight!"

Cap steps forward, leading all of the forces behind him. Across the field, the Persian infantry marches towards them. Cap searches within himself and finds the rage held within. This time, he won't wait to release it. His vision reddens, and he feels suppression as he forces himself not to run into battle. The two armies get about twenty five yards apart. Cap can't wait any longer. He rushes in, his army behind him.

The two armies clash, blood flying into the air as men are slain immediately. Cap's army seems to take on the entire Persian army. He and his men fight hard, but the Persian army is just too many. They are falling men left and right, but they are still getting pushed back. Cap doesn't attempt to urge his men forward. They are all just fighting for their lives.

"Fall back!" Cap yells between enemies, knowing that if he waits too much longer his strategy will fail miserably.

He doesn't have time to look around, but the sound of screaming from both sides tells him he's fallen back to Cuchulain and Heracles. The Persian force is still too large though, and he continues to fall back. With both of their flanks being attacked, the Persians begin to cram in on each other. They don't seem to notice, still believing in their sheer size, and the belief that the weak force in front of them will crumble at any time. Behind the Persian army, Cap can see the armies of Agartha and Atlantis close in from behind. There is no longer an escape for the enemy.

"Now!" Cap yells, releasing his men to push forward.

He and his men stop moving back, and begin fighting harder. They fight *their* way now. The eyes of the Persian men grow fearful as their movement gets more and more restricted. Their officers try to yell out orders, but to no avail. What had seemed like a sure victory is now beginning to look like a sure loss. In desperation, they begin to attack themselves. Little by little, they fight each other for any means of escape.

Across the field, the three commanders watch in horror. Breanna, Martine, and Luke just stare in disbelief. The Persian army outnumbered their enemy by at least three to one. Yet, they managed to surround the great army. It is becoming a very bloody massacre! Slowly, Luke's face reddens at the sight, and stares at the one person that is causing the catastrophe. Cap.

For Martine, it had seemed too easy. Outnumbered and over powered, they were supposed to flee, surrender, or lose by a decisive victory. Now, because of this one man, they are on the verge of losing the battle! It is inconceivable. It just doesn't seem possible! How he was able, in just a matter of moments, form a battle plan and use it against them? It is unbelievable!

Breanna, however, looks on in surprise and with admiration. The horror of what she is seeing doesn't escape her notice, but the skill and tactics that are being used are too great to be unaccounted for. Never before has she been challenged as much as a commander. After she had sent a squad of vampires to the cities below, just to search for Cap, they never returned. Now she knows why. Looking across the field, she begins to hope that her adversary lives. She smiles at the thought. He is making her a better strategist, and she likes the feeling of it.

The battle in front of her ceases. Cap's army just stops. She can see the feathers on Cap's helmet moving towards her direction. The army around him cheers as he walks through them. Breanna smiles at the sight. He survived the impossible odds. She may just have the opportunity to face him in battle again.

Cap stands in front of his combined forces facing the vampires and werecats. The battle isn't over, just a brief stop in the fighting. Behind him, a lone Persian soldier stands up silently. Raising a dagger over his head, he brings it down into Cap's shoulder. Cap hit's the ground in pain. Filled with rage, he spins around and catches the soldier between the legs with Adflictus. With a strength he's never felt, he catapults the man across the field. The man lands and bounces between Breanna and Martine. He slides to a stop, where he lays still.

Cap pulls the dagger out of his shoulder, blood flowing after. A tingling sensation is felt over the injured area, and Cap smiles. The imps are doing their job well. They must have saved hundreds of lives by now. He can feel his shoulder itch as the wound begins to close. After a moment, the feeling is gone.

He continues to stand, staring at Breanna and her forces. He can't help but wonder what she has in store for his forces next. The sound of a wolf's howl draws his attention to the North. Turning to look, he sees about a thousand wolves running towards him. Cap smiles, he couldn't have asked for a better time for them to arrive. Behind them, a thunderstorm follows.

He greets Adolf and Logan as they walk up to him, "Welcome, my friends! I'm glad to see that you could make it."

"It looks like we missed all the fun," Logan says sarcastically to him.

"It isn't over yet," Cap tells him, "This was only the beginning."

"What happened here?" Adolf asks.

"The Persian army," Diamondback says walking up to them, "I don't know where you got that idea from, but holy hell did it work," he says to Cap.

"It is called Battle Annihilation," Cap tells them all, "I took it from something I learned from Hannibal. He used the same tactic against the Romans. We won't be able to use it again."

"Pity," Logan says, "That did some serious damage."

"Yeah," Cap says cautiously looking around. "Logan, can you have Heracles and Cuchulain keep the men ready. This isn't over yet, and I have a feeling that Breanna has more up her sleeve. Diamondback and Adolf? Let's go see if they would like to renegotiate."

Cap is about walk across the field, but he sees Breanna moving towards him. Behind her, the werecats and vampires follow her. Cap's forces now outnumber hers, so he isn't too worried about that aspect. Except that…

A gigantic army tops the hill behind Breanna. He can see a full infantry, cavalry, and war elephants. As the army marches over the hill that had hidden it, Cap can see that his forces are outnumbered once again. The sight of it alone makes him shake with worry. His worries transform into anger. He should have known that something like this would unfold.

His army lines up in ranks behind him. The smell of fear fills the air. A few scared souls run out of the area. Cap doesn't blame them. He would probably join them if he were in their situation. That is, if his pride would allow him to. He has to stay and fight. This war could end on this night. In fact, he is sure of it.

Thunderstorms now begin to surround the entire area from all directions. The winds begin to swirl around with hurricane force speeds. The south brings in a salty mist from the ocean. The north brings a freezing cold wind from the north. The eastern storm shows signs of hail, and the western storm shows signs of tornadoes. In the center of it all, the full moon sits in the center of the sky, gazing down upon the battle that is about to unfold. The clouds surround it, but don't cover it. The moon's light shines down on the forces. The only constant light in the sky. The signs of all the storms are an ominous sign that this battle will be horrific. The winds from the four storms swirl around the area. The rain doesn't seem to hit the ground, but circles around hitting everyone and everything horizontally.

"Now, *I'm* worried," Diamondback says, his voice shaking slightly.

Cap turns around and yells though the wind and thunder, "We can end this tonight! We fight for those who can't and for those who have! We fight to preserve our ways of life! For our freedoms! For our choices! Tonight, we will force *them* to surrender to us! Whatever our fates may be, we will show them that they will never, NEVER, control our destinies!" The armies cheer and call out their battle cries at his words. They challenge their enemies with them, in defiance to what the opposing force stands for.

"Breanna is mine," Cap says with determination, more to himself than anyone else.

"Leave Luke to me," Diamondback says with an evil smile upon his face, "We have an unsettled score to finish. I'll make sure that little piss ant learns some manners."

Breanna points at Cap. Cap points back with Adflictus, "You're on!" he yells.

Both armies rush at each other, splitting into groups. Cap and Diamondback lead Cap's forces into Breanna and Luke's. Adolf lets out a howl and charges the werewolves into the werecats. The armies of Cuchulain, the Knights of the Round Table, Heracles, Butukhan, and Anastasios clash with the gigantic army.

Breanna rushes Cap, pulling out a gladius sword. Cap doesn't slow down. Their weapons hit each other with tremendous force, creating thunder of their own and knocking both of them to the ground. Two vampires grab Cap and hold him as Breanna attempts to thrust her gladius into Cap's heart. Cap pulls hard to the left, and Breanna's thrust pierces her own vampire's heart. Someone pulls the vampire off Cap. 'To hell with this!' he thinks. He opens his mind and a stream of fire flows out from the pebble on his chest. It encircles Breanna and Cap, creating a wall of fire that no creature can penetrate. He swings at Breanna as she pulls the gladius out of the vampire corpse. She blocks the blow just in time, knocking her backwards.

They rush in on each other, swinging and stabbing. With each block and evasion, they're battle becomes more personal. Neither can seem to get an advantage. Breanna's vampiric abilities don't seem to faze the mortal, nor does Cap's heightened abilities with his rage do any damage to the vampire. As each gets to an advantage, the wall of fire's heat seems to give the opponent added courage and strength.

Breanna swings hard and wide, slicing through the fire and killing vampires and humans alike. Cap blocks the blow. Turning around swinging, the mace of Adflictus hits her gladius. The gladius twists around her extended arm, slicing her sleeve. Furious, she swings, thrusts, and slices faster than Cap has ever seen. He manages to block the attacks. Ducking under a thrust, he swings Adflictus into her abdomen. The curve lands, knocking her backwards.

She moves in again, unfazed by the blow. She feints a swing, slicing down as Cap tries to evade. The blow glances off his shield, slicing into his leg. Angered beyond explanation, Cap begins attacking Breanna with lightning speed. The speed catches her off guard, and she can only block his attacks. Cap begins pushing her back, angering her more.

Finding an opening, Breanna evades Cap's swinging attack. She turns and swings as Cap does the same. The two weapons hit each other with thunder. Flying out of their hands, the weapons land out of reach in the fighting. Circling each other, the sounds of fighting around them grows fiercer. Breanna flies at Cap, picking him up by his shoulders, and flies straight up into the air.

Fear grips Cap as the thought of falling to the ground enters his head. Not waiting to be dropped, he swings his legs up, and then throws them down with all his strength. The force pulls her down unexpectedly. They fall to the ground with increasing speed. They fight in the air, trying to gain an advantage on each other as they fall. Neither can get the upper hand. Lightning strikes the ground under them just before they land. They are forced away from each other, and land hard. They get up slowly, ready for an attack from the other.

"This won't be over tonight," Breanna says suddenly, "It is a stalemate. I'll pull my forces back, for now, as long as you do the same."

"I'm not pulling my forces out of anywhere," Cap replies angrily.

"Don't worry, we *will* meet again," she says to him, looking around at the fighting, "This war isn't going to end tonight." She yells something out that Cap doesn't understand, and flies into the air. As the shock of her leaving hits him, the flames surrounding him flow back into the pebble.

The remaining vampires follow her out of sight. The sound of cheering is heard to his left. He can see the army Breanna brought retreating. Wolf howls to his right gives him the understanding that the werecats have pulled out also. In front of him, he can see Diamondback with two small xiphos swords in his hands walking towards him, breathing very hard.

"Damn, that brother of yours sure can run in cat form," Diamondback says when he gets close enough, "It looks like we won."

"But we didn't," Cap says with disappointment, "This isn't over yet. I don't think it will ever be over. You should have seen Breanna's face. I think she enjoys these encounters. I don't think this can be over until either her or me, maybe both of us, are dead."

Cap looks around as his forces come together around him. The size has been cut down to almost half. As the sky begins to clear, stars can be seen through the clearing clouds. The lightning ceases, and the wind and rain stops. He looks down at the blood soaked ground. 'Too many lives,' he thinks to himself, 'and it isn't over yet.'

"She had us," he says softly, raising his head.

"I'm sorry?" Diamondback says with confusion.

"She had us," Cap says again, "I wasn't willing to back down, or back down our army. If she had stayed, this could have been over tonight."

"So what can we do?" Diamondback asks.

"Whatever we can," Cap answers, "Train, recruit, change tactics as much as possible so they can't predict what we'll do, or anything else. We need to persevere and win. We need to outlast them. We need more people. We have to do everything possible not to lose." He looks around at all the bodies lying upon the ground. "We can't lose," he says very quietly.

He walks away without another word. He walks through the men towards the rising sun. He stops when he is alone. He looks back at the men behind him. Turning back, he hits his knees and mourns for the lives lost. A kneeling shadow silhouette in the rising sunlight.

List Mythical Creatures

(In Alphabetical Order)

Agoolik:	*An Inuit ice spirit that aids hunters and fishermen. though the spirit doesn't aid Cap, it is deemed benevolent.*
Cacus:	*A Roman fire breathing giant. In mythology, this giant was killed by Heracles.*
Gods:	*Immortal beings of mythology. Different religions had different gods for different purposes in nature.*
Heroes:	*Offspring of gods and humans, heroes have special Supernatural abilities from their deity parents.*
Ifrit:	*An Arabian fire genie. Although information is scarce on this creature, it is mentioned in the Koran <u>Sura</u> <u>An-Naml</u> (27:39-40)*
Imp:	*A demonic servant similar to fairies and demons, they are mischievous, small, and can be manipulated to do good.*
Leviathan:	*The Jewish sea monster. Mentioned in the Old Testament of the Bible, this sea creature has many different descriptions. Some believe that it was a living dinosaur.*
Pterippus:	*Greek winged horse. Pegasus, the most famous, is of this species.*
Titans:	*Greek giant beings that ruled the world before the gods.*
Vampire:	*Of Slavic origins, they are the undead that subsist on blood.*
Werecat:	*A cat-human shape shifter.*
Werewolf:	*A wolf-human shape shifter.*
Zombie:	*A reanimated corpse. Undead and sometimes decomposing.*

Made in the USA
Las Vegas, NV
10 September 2021